D1553860

GIRLS *of* ALEXANDRIA

GIRLS *of* ALEXANDRIA

Edwar al-Kharrat

Translated by
Frances Liardet

QUARTET BOOKS

First published in English by Quartet Books Limited 1993
A member of the Namara Group
27/29 Goodge Street, London W1P 1FD

Copyright © by Edwar al-Kharrat
Translation copyright © by Frances Liardet 1993

British Library cataloguing in publication data

Kharrat, Edwar al–
Girls of Alexandria
I. Title
892.736 [F]

ISBN 0 7043 7006 9

Phototypeset by Intype, London
Printed and bound in Great Britain by Bookcraft (Bath) Ltd

FIC
KHARRAT
E

Contents

Introduction

Edwar al-Kharrat was born in Alexandria in 1926 into a Coptic Christian family. His mother came from a village near Alexandria and his father from Upper Egypt. His father, who owned a small business, died in 1943, obliging al-Kharrat to earn a living while completing his studies in order to support his family. In 1946 he graduated in Law from Alexandria University. From 1948–50 he was detained for belonging to a left-wing revolutionary movement. Upon his release he worked until 1955 for an insurance company in Alexandria. In 1959, when his first collection of short stories was published, he joined the Afro-Asian Peoples' Solidarity Organisation and the Afro-Asian Writers' Union. Edwar al-Kharrat's writing first began to receive critical acclaim in the sixties and for a period he edited the famous literary magazine *Galiri 68*. He now lives in Cairo, and his published work to date includes novels, short stories, translations and essays.

Girls of Alexandria takes us back to the world celebrated in al-Kharrat's earlier novel, *City of Saffron* (Quartet, 1989); that is to say, the Alexandria of the thirties and forties where al-Kharrat grew up. However, the narrator is not al-Kharrat but his protagonist Mikha'il – and Mikha'il's reminiscences are not the author's autobiography but the most subtly crafted fiction. The streets and shorelines familiar to the reader of *City of Saffron* are here frequented by a Mikha'il who is for the most part slightly older than in the earlier book – although the narration weaves and loops, like memory does, back to his earliest childhood days. In *Girls of Alexandria* we learn more about Mikha'il the adolescent, the student, the young adult. He prints revolutionary pamphlets in secret, he marches in anti-Government demonstrations; he meets a British sailor and tests him out on *The Tempest*. As a poverty-stricken student he calculates his family's expenditure (cooking oil, tap washers) down to the last millieme; as the employee of a building firm he haunts cafés and nightclubs until the small hours. The post-revolution exodus takes many of his friends from Alexandria and when he meets them years later in Beirut or London it is not only their faces which have changed.

The girls of Alexandria inhabit every corner of his beloved city. They are as various as women can be; there is Mona his neighbour, Susu the schoolgirl at the tram-stop; there is the Madonna he encounters in the potters' yard. There is Sylvana harried into wartime prostitution, Nagiya whose baby shares his name, Rawiya the near-feral girl-child of the oasis. The story of his encounter with each of these girls is punctuated by effusions of poetic, visionary prose. The deeds of heroines from books and films, childhood adventures, news articles past and present, and the voices of people long dead are all mingled together in these passages. At one point scraps of adolescent poetry jostle with price lists for dry goods and quotations from Keats and Shakespeare; cleverly, this passage turns out to be taken straight from old business papers which Mikha'il re-used after his father's death by filling every spare margin with writing of his own. They are not so much streams of consciousness as torrents of the subconscious; and they are saturated with the presence, not of any particular one of these Alexandrian girls, but of the one woman who is all of them. 'However many she is, she is one: however fleeting, she is eternal.'

And there is the key to the text, for so is Alexandria at once fleeting and eternal. It seems that Mikha'il can't stop talking about Alexandria. It is almost as if *City of Saffron* and *Girls of Alexandria* are two excursions into a discourse which continues unbroken, freed from the constraints of a linear narrative and therefore from time. The shade of the streets, the multiple colours of the sea, the façades of the houses on the Corniche are vividly recalled by Mikha'il, as are the rooms long-deserted by the people he loved – the divan, the rug, the cushion, the coffee-pot exhaling North African spices. The rain, streaming across the panes or beating against the shutters; the taste of butter biscuits. All these belong in the city of the past, and yet they are ever-present. In the fifth chapter this timelessness is made explicit in a paean to the Alexandria where every quarter, landmark and monument is referred to by both its Greek and its Arabic names. The text, fragmented as it is by sweet nightmarish visions, illustrates the tension between transient surface experience and the unending dream of life which underpins it. To talk about Alexandria is to talk about just this dream, with all its loves, losses and pains. The story of each Alexandrian girl is but one facet of Mikha'il's encounter with the one woman who inhabits the dream. She is the life force without beginning or end, the ultimate reality.

'The dream has no time. It is no dream. There is no time.'

Frances Liardet

Glossary

Amm	lit. 'uncle', title for a man (for example, Amm Bashir the doorman)
Effendi	title for a man (for example, Gabra Effendi the teacher) and term of address – 'Sir'
foul-beans	large brown-skinned broad beans usually cooked in oil, a staple food
haret	alley
shari'	street
siga	a game similar to noughts and crosses
tarboosh	a dark red brimless felt cap with a high flat crown and black tassel
Umm	lit. 'mother', title for a woman (for example, Mahmud's mother will be known as Umm Mahmud)

O girls of Alexandria
You love your seaside promenade
In silky clothes with lacy trim
Your lips are sugar-sweet

Girls of Alexandria, multiple, single, peerless: who are you? I have never met you face to face but I know you like a lover: and no one knows more than a lover.

Paradise-girls of memory and fantasy, appearing ever in bodies and souls gone and forgotten now. Reveries aeons old, they throng my boyhood, youth, my later years: even now they undulate through my dreams with a life more carnal than that of any woman.

Girls of Alexandria, sea of Alexandria: constant unending seduction: affection which cannot perish.

However many she is, she is one: however fleeting, she is eternal.

How can I resist her?

1

Bird of Youth Alighting upon the Sea

It is as if I am entering the house in *haret* el-Gullanar once more. In through the narrow doorway and on to the dim stone staircase in one stride.

And it is as if I can sense Mona there, bursting with life, behind the door of the ground-floor flat on the right.

A bit older than me still. Going out in the morning to Rosa the Syrian's workshop in Gheit el-Enab and returning only at the end of the afternoon. Her sister Gamalat came back a little later from the spinning-mill in Karmuz.

Before the holidays began, when I came home from school every day, her door would open just as I reached the stairs. In that small ground-floor hallway, in that tiny fleeting moment between the afternoon's vanishing and the dampish gloom of the entrance, I caught the glimmer of her face.

Her dress skimmed her knees, falling loosely down over her rounded thighs. I was aware also of her small bosom, free and firm and rising as she lifted her face to me. She looked at me with her slanted, slightly bulging eyes. A look at once bashful and bold, a look which made my heart flutter; I did not know what it meant. Softly she said: 'Hello', her voice trembling and yet entirely confident. She all but brushed against me as she went out into the alley, dragging her down-at-heel slippers, exciting me with the rustle of her dress and the smell of her newly washed skin.

But now it was the long summer holiday and these days I didn't see her until I went up to the roof-terrace at sunset. I watched out for her through the window, with Keats in English in my hand – *La Belle Dame Sans Merci*, from the *Golden Dragon Anthology* – until I spotted her at the end of the street. Then the blood surged in my heart.

That boy who I was, who I am still! So romantic, fired by his sexuality's overpowering awakening – and thinking himself naïve all at once!

I loved Mona, but could not be certain that she loved me, or anything of the kind.

As if I had forgotten it, Keats and the *Golden Dragon* was still in my hand as I pushed open the wooden door to the roof-terrace. I was struck by the light of the end of the day, the slightly sharp moisture in the air from the breeze off the nearby salt-lake – slightly sharp and slightly putrid as well, from the street smells.

The big drake came rushing towards me, darting out his neck and hissing in hot defence of the kingdom I was invading.

Mona was sitting cross-legged on the tiles. The mother duck was under her thigh, gently pinned beneath the dark smooth flesh. She had the duck's flat yellow bill grasped in one dripping-wet hand and with the other she was cramming in pellets of bran mixed with millet paste. The ducklings ran gaily all over the terrace, shining, bobbing, sauntering around, balls of fluff with big red bills.

She had changed. Her summer housedress had ridden up to show her graceful thighs. The material was soaked around the neckline and clung to her bare skin, outlining the bumps of little breasts snuggled solidly in wetness. I could not tear my gaze away from the depth of the coveted obscurity between her thighs, that dim place which now and then fleetingly glimmered more clearly lit and brightly coloured even in secrecy.

I heard my own voice, a bit choked and hoarse. 'Hey, Mona. I want to see you.'

She looked up at me without letting go of the flat gaping duck's bill. Her short pitch-black hair was uncombed and sprang into its natural curl. For the first time I could clearly see a hollow scar on her pointed chin, a thin line paler than the soft brown skin on either side.

Beneath the slight puffiness of her lids her eyes seemed oddly full – and serious too, belying her bantering tone. 'Well aren't you looking at me right now, dear? God keep your eyes safe and sound! Oh – and may good health look on you as well! May you never have sight of trouble!'

I was nonplussed by this, and could not immediately reply.

She had already stood me up twice, though they weren't definite appointments; once at Shallalat, and then at the end of our street where it met *shari'* Raghib Pasha.

In another time I said that I did not want you to bear the burden of my silence, that I did not want you to entrench yourself away from me behind this silence. And was the silence ever broken? Did we ever really meet?

I said: Despair tells me that we did not.

I do not believe it, I do not have it in me to believe it but it is persistent, it has a crushing logic.

The bird of youth wheels on a dark skyline far away from me. It is as if I grasp it in my hands and it flutters against my fingers.

Finally I managed to persuade her to come and meet me in front of the fish market at Maks on Thursday at five. Afterwards she would go straight on to her aunt's in Sayyala.

Mona told me that her aunt was a lot younger than her mother. She had come to her grandmother late in life. She had been married for years to a foreman at the harbour, but had never had a baby. Mona had told me that her aunt had tried all the remedies. She had worn every charm there was; she had visited the tomb of St Abu Dardar; she had tried spells and talismans and black magic. She had chanted and danced together with the other women and sacrificed at the shrines of holy men. She had even gone to Cairo to place her hands on the tombs of the saints and righteous there, to sweep the floor at the mosque of Our Lady Zaynab, and to hammer nails into the gateway at Bab Zuweila and into the tree of the Virgin Mary at Mattareya as well – but even now she still had not had a child. Mona told me that she had been prescribed the fresh blood of a turtle slaughtered as it came out of the water.

Mona's face shone and her small teeth gleamed as she chatted away.

I had told myself that I wouldn't think of getting involved with her. I would never go and see her. I would not wait for her to come to me in any place on earth, neither accidentally nor by design. And I broke this promise to myself.

And I could never have forgotten, not for one moment, that loving look in her slightly bulging eyes; eyes filled with rapture, as if the world were not there, as she lifted her face to her cousin Mahrus. Tall, thick-lipped Mahrus, who lived in a property on the Piazza beyond *shari'* No. 12.

Neither could I forget the demolition of my heart, or the agonies of a passion which was overshadowed by futility and flourished unsuppressed at the same time.

Nor has my callow heart stopped throbbing, though it has long known an almost unbearable pain.

Then I laughed a little inside – I do still – at the tales of this heart of mine, though they are utterly earnest – though they are bitter in my mouth.

It was after the Friday noon prayer that Nefisa's voice was suddenly heard in the alley. 'Hear me, good people!' she was calling. 'Hear me, I say to summon you – Mona! Umm Mahmud's daughter!' There was a challenge in her voice which could not be ignored. Her calls were weighed down by the staggering burden of the scorching sun.

'Hear me, Mona my dear! Come out or I'll show you up! Come out girl!'

'Come, Mahmud, you prince among men! See what your sister, name of God upon her, has done!'

'Very well. Show your love discreetly but hide your hate completely. When the sun comes up you can see who's been put to shame, my dear, my darling. Think of it! In broad daylight! Imagine! Making a complete spectacle of herself! Everybody hear me!'

All the windows of the alley opened, clattering one after the other against the walls. The panes of glass, stuck over with wide strips of yellow paper, came swinging out back to back. Even in that oppressive noon-day heat all the boys and girls came straight out in the faded shifts they wore next to the skin. 'Come off it, Nefisa!' they shouted as they raced each other into the street. 'Give over, do!'

Nefisa could be seen from the waist up. Her small bosom, finely-formed and perfectly round, was gathered up so that it almost spilled out as she leaned out of her window. She was coffee-coloured with clear skin and a very smooth, shiny face. Her thick jet-black hair was cropped to curl around her head. She was as small as a young girl; you wouldn't think she was more than twelve until you saw her firm bust pushing up the narrow always-shiny yoke of the dress which hugged her belly so tightly. Her dainty form was completely feminine, firm and taut without an ounce of flabbiness. The mature gaze of her big eyes shone from the smooth darkness of her face. Her ample mouth pouted sensually. We all knew that Mona and Nefisas were best friends, soul-mates in fact, and that they both loved Mahrus, who worked with Mona's elder brother in a workshop near the Piazza. Mahrus who came and had supper with them nearly every evening. I didn't hate Mahrus – but this is not to say that I forgave him.

When I heard Nefisa scream I began to quake. She was notorious. No one could insinuate, defame, sow rumours or bellow from the rooftops the way Nefisa could. Her father, the carriage-driver Ma'allem Abu Dera'a – we were all aware of this – held sway in the quarter. He had a long arm when it came to matters of opium and hashish and the women from the brothels at Kom Bikir; there was no one who didn't have to reckon with him.

And when it came to the fine classical art of street-slanging, the queen of the quarter, of the whole neighbourhood, was his daughter Nefisa. I had a feeling that the day would not end happily.

I ran to the window. My mother called my sisters back – 'Shameless girls!' – but I could see immediately that the window belonging to Umm Mahmud, Mona's mother, was closed. The familiar dark blue paper tacked to the frame, faded a little now by the sun, completely covered the tight-shut panes. I could actually feel the tension behind them; from where I stood above them I could actually feel the presence emanating from Mona's body, her mother hanging on to her by her hands, by her whole arms, to stop her going outside . . .

Umm Mahmud was the only person who was still in the habit of mentioning that her late husband – God rest his soul – had been an official of some standing in the municipality. She still had a picture of him in the drawing-room, clad in a formal suit and a *tarboosh*. It hung in the exact middle of the wall, above the never-used dining table which was spread with an embroidered cloth ingrained with the dust of years. In the middle of the table there was a stemmed glass dish made of genuine crystal and filled with wax fruit – oranges, bananas and tangerines. And there was a set of flaking gilt chairs ranged against the walls, like an ancient squad of retired guards, all around the room.

I knew that room, the way it looked in the gloom, with the windows shut and Mona beside me. I knew it so well.

Umm Mahmud gave me preserved dates when I visited. She brought them out from the kitchen, each fruit soaked in its syrup, moist and succulent. She was a skinny, dried-up little body but very good-hearted. She never missed a prayer-time. Old and worn out, she silently served her three children with the light of her eyes.

By now Nefisa had exhausted the traditional preamble she had by heart: 'Who do you think you are, you rusty needle, you skinny drumstick, on the heap with you', etc., etc. It was time to move on to the second half, which was of her own invention.

I watched her run down and out into the alley. She was barefoot. The children were silent now. They clustered with bated breath around her.

Without a pause she threw herself down on the ground. Her tight dress rode up a little to reveal her dark thighs with their strong, glistening muscles. She began to moan and call out. It was completely abandoned, unmistakably lecherous. 'Mahrus!' she called, her voice fairly melting with lustful entreaty.

Mona it was who lay flung down in the dust of her desire for all the world to see.

The children who had come hotfoot from the neighbouring streets had been joined by respectable men in traditional long tunics and light coats, by urchins from *shari'* Raghib Pasha, by women whose clinging black shawls slipped from their shoulders. There were a few peals of laughter, hurried whispers, and the odd momentary frown. Then everyone was quietly agog. The noonday heat beat down on us and we stood as if petrified beneath it. The writhing came first; moans of lust pierced the absolute silence. Then the moment of penetration, the lethal convulsion, the agony of her scream as she reached the pinnacle of pleasure. And finally a cry which trailed off into torpid stillness.

It was an obscenity so blatant that it reached the limit of obscenity and defeated itself. Now it hardly provoked revulsion, or anger, or even the laughter brought on by embarrassment or the desire to ward off evil. Rather the obscenity had turned into an intricate magic possessed of an incomprehensible, inexplicable power. A sense of maleness filled and oppressed the whole alley. The midday heat was awash with it. It had become primal, pure, and innocent once more.

She jumped to her feet, this girl who had dissolved into the body of her beloved friend and enemy. She jumped up and let out a scream which struck the entire alley dumb with astonishment and alarm. She began to twist her slight form this way and

7

that; skilfully she began to writhe, this time in the toils of labour. She howled with the agony of a mother about to give birth. Then, lo and behold, she was holding the new-born in her arms. We heard it give its first faint cry. We saw it, every one of us, with our own eyes, a tiny red-skinned thing with eyes shut. In the harsh noon light she bared her breast, she really did; she pressed two fingers against the dark virgin flesh of her round breast and suckled him. 'Hush now, hush now,' she chanted. 'Sleep . . .'

Then she was transformed again into Nefisa. Nefisa came out of the concealing veil of Mona's body. Once more she began to scream at Mona. 'Where did you take the child, you whore!' she cried. 'Come here, Mahrus, and find out where your son is! She's tucked it away somewhere – come and find out where, my darling! You can't fall pregnant and breastfeed and have nothing to show for it – the truth will come out in the end, Miss Mooo-na!'

By now the crowd had started to move. The spell was broken. Her father's wife, Sitt Saniya, came down and hid Nefisa behind her own wobbly stoutness. The other women of the street gathered round. Together they tried to get her to go inside, crying out, whispering in her ear, embracing and patting her. 'My dear, in the name of God, the Merciful, the Compassionate . . . by the Prophet, may our words be acceptable to them below. May this evil miss its mark. Enough, my dear, it's over. You two are like sisters, my love, you can't do without each other. Can't be parted – like a body and its shadow. Come on, my dear, that's enough. Up you get . . .' And all the while Umm Mahmud's window was silent, shut fast on her injured honour, a stubborn defence for her unearned disgrace.

It was sacrilege. And I was the one brought down and wounded.

No remission ever from the obduracy of this world. Absolute finality. Nothing can counter it. Nothing can explain it.

The pulse of my blood throbs in the desolation and the silence. How cruel is the pain of it.

8

My tears never dry, nor do they cease to fall. They concern no one.

When Nefisa stood up her slight frame was still trembling slightly as if she could not help it. Her green dress was dusty where she filled it out, still shiny in the hollow of her slim waist. She broke free of the women whose tender murmurs, tinny cries and muttered gloating still filled the air. 'Really, my dear, you can't betray friendship just like that. Only a low sort would do that, and you're a well-brought up girl and so is Mona. Isn't she a sister to you – a fine, well-bred girl? What is this? . . .'

But Nefisa slipped out of the embracing arms alone. I saw the silent tears flowing slowly down her round face. The flushed darkness was gone, to be replaced by a pallor worthy of a virgin on her deathbed. She was alone.

Fallen, heartrent, on fire with rage, I knew that I loved Mona and that I would not stop loving her for one moment. I quelled my soul's misgivings, I tamed its unbridled temptations. I heaped reproach on myself, charged myself with laxity and yet I knew that I would be her constant lover to the end. Furthermore I knew that as far as she was concerned betrayal had no meaning, no existence, that the clamour of this ferocious pain was a revelation striking me to my heart's core.

The sea was wide. Small fishing boats with narrow sails were bobbing on a deep blue swell so gentle as to be almost flat. I saw that the fishermen, in their waistcoats and wide enfolding black breeches, were spreading their nets to shake out the sardines. The fish rained down, tumbling and colliding with soft thick thumps to fall in a silvery heap, quivering still with life, in the bottom of the boat. The men were stooping to throw the small fish back. Sunburned boys swam around the boats, some making do with droopy drawers of rough cotton on the verge of slipping off, others stark naked, all ducking headfirst underwater. When they came up again they each had a shivering, squirming, flipping, slipping fish in their hands which they tossed into pouches run up from canvas, dark wet canvas which poured water each time they broke the surface. Grey gulls with big strong wings swooped suddenly down from on high to snatch their prey from the boats and from the boys' hands – boys whose hollow chests heaved continually so that the skin shone taught over their jutting bones – and then they soared triumphantly away, straight up into the air, with a menacing scream of anger or of fear.

It was a little while after this that my father died, but I knew already that my mother would come down here to get this small-fry for us, a great cheap load of it, for . . . how much? Three quarters – or was it a whole piastre?

I had taken the tram for Maks, the one which was open on both sides. Love, jealousy and humiliation held me in a vice. My pain had the sharp, rotten smell of the tanneries which had choked me as we passed. I wasn't sure if she would come, so I had made up my mind to be late. I had dallied over every possible thing and then left for the main town station at what I thought was a gentle stroll, but I soon realized that I had lengthened my stride – indeed I was hurrying at such a pace that I managed to bump into the few passers-by. I made a dash for the first tram but let it pass, only to go nearly mad with anxiety when the following one was late.

It was down by the big petroleum tanks, where there was a leaping column of flame which never went out, that I saw the Afrikaaner soldiers. Powerful-looking, armed to the teeth, they were standing with their backs to us in a tense line on the beach, staring out to sea. The English battleship towered white and immovable on the water. It had its guns trained on a smaller warship, and even at that distance I could make out the Greek letters on the side and the red flag which fluttered from the pole as if it were defying death. And I saw a line of soldiers in helmets and transparent bullet-proof masks, soldiers bristling with weapons, blocking the narrow streets trodden by prophets and poets and dreamers in Jerusalem and Ramallah and Nazareth and al-Khalil, raking the crowds of children with machine-gun fire and hurling tear-gas cylinders. Soldiers surrounding the round granite monument which gleams by night in the middle of Tahrir Square, beating boys and girls with truncheons, spiriting prisoners of war away into stifling locked railway carriages bound for the mired and frozen trenches of Warsaw and Siberia and the gas-chambers of Dachau. Soldiers harrying the crowds of workers from the spinning- and weaving-mills in Mahalla, Kafr al-Dawar, Karmuz, hounding the students of law, medicine and all the other faculties on Abbasiya Hill in Muharram Bey. Their small yellow tanks knew what they had to do; they shot bullets from their old-fashioned long cannons and hundreds fell in the great square outside the Winter Palace; the sirens of their black cars wailed as they were barricaded in front of the Sorbonne; they dragged trained and vicious dogs by their leather leads to maul black legs in Johannesburg or by the Mississippi. Many years later I was to learn that the English had killed hundreds of revolutionary seamen who had joined the liberation army in Greece, and that they had imprisoned the rest so that the revolution collapsed after the war.

Alighting at the last stop I discovered from the tram-driver that it was still only five to five. By now I was convinced that she would not come. I stood, unable to grasp completely what was happening to me, by the old Citadel wall. On my left the big grey stones rose above me; I had the impression that they were holding themselves fast against collapse. I stared unseeingly at the stallholders and fishermen squatting by their wares – baskets of all shapes and sizes brimming with sardines, grey mullet, speckled scallops, prawns and crabs. I took care not to step on the little discarded fish which lay squashed on the pavement. Their flattened white bodies bulged with little pinkish bloody bumps, bumps all over the bellies and heads which had been smashed flush with the ground . . .

Everything seemed to be looming at me in a menacing

11

fashion. The dark green boards of the Zephyr Café, the cloudy windowpanes gleaming at me from a short distance away. The shed by the railway crossing which bore a sign saying 'Thabit Thabit and Co., Natural Chilean Nitrates' in large tall-stroked ornamental letters. These words had provoked constant dreams ever since the days of my visits to the Zephyr Café with my uncle Nathan, when we used to come and eat fish with lemon and onion and spices hot from the oven in greaseproof paper. The house was the one with ornate Arab balconies which I was to recognize forty years later, changed and deserted-looking though it was by then. And the Seagull Hotel – there was no arabesquely elegant restaurant in those days, just a sand-coloured building whose murky secrets were locked away behind the blank walls.

Even now the smell of salt, fresh fish and the sea's iodine assails me.

A rowdy band of Australian soldiers in wide-brimmed hats got down out of a gharry in front of the café. They were whistling at the girls and women walking by with their clingy black shawls drawn tight over their bottoms. 'Come on, bint!' they shouted unconcernedly, almost carelessly. 'Fantasia! Come on!' Why did I tell her to come here, I thought.

My heart gave one single lurch when I saw her. She was standing with a fisherman, a very tall young man with a hand-some sunbrowned face and blue eyes. He was leaning over a tub filled with brine. A large captive turtle, still alive, was thrashing sluggishly within its copper walls. When I came to a halt nearby she didn't turn to greet me. I thought: 'She's afraid that someone will see us together.' Then I thought: 'She has denied me thrice.'

She was bargaining with the fisherman in her slightly nasal voice, looking up at him with her beguiling gaze. 'No holds barred,' I thought. 'Femininity is the only weapon she knows.' Her long fingers played around her bare throat as she fiddled with the big beads of her necklace.

12

'No, my friend,' she was saying. 'Ten piastres is an awful lot, by the Prophet. Give it to me for five and I'll only buy from you, I won't go to anyone else. By the Prophet and Him who made the Prophet a prophet, truly, I only want to do you a favour. I might climb down for the sake of your nice manners and because you're a fine lad – go on, sell, and God will reward you . . .'

'All right, enough sweet talk!' he said, this splendid Alexandrian boy. 'Just tell me where you live, princess, and I'll deliver to your door. We've all got to help each other, after all . . . It's all Providence in the end.'

She didn't mention that the turtle wasn't for her. She had left the door of temptation open for him, I thought. She had a way of doing that.

She darted a look at me from the corner of her eye. I felt it drown me in a hot, troubled, impure flood; it was a look which banished me, denied me, made me nothing. At that moment I realized she was going to turn me into a cipher in a dance of numbers the sum of which I could not compute. She would drain the blood from me; I already felt myself to be a flat and one-dimensional ghost, a voiceless thing. I knew then and there how she would tell Nefisa, how Nefisa in turn would secretly tell my sister Aida – who would hesitate a great deal, who was afraid to speak until I calmed her down and allayed her fears: 'I don't know what I'm going to do about that schoolboy, the son of those Copts upstairs. So he's in love with me! Isn't that nice! Aren't I lucky! The way he talks to me, my dear, sometimes that's very nice too and other times I can't make head or tail . . . He loves me? It's just a lot of babble! So what? So Mahrus will get cross, darn it, that's what. What to do about that boy! . . .'

The sun flamed as it sank beneath the horizon. Mona walked on, ignoring me, moving away from me under the ancient wall of the Citadel. The young fisherman was with her. He was pushing a cart bearing the copper tub and the captive turtle.

13

Her face glowed from the heat, the sting of the sea-breeze and the nearness of the young man whom she had conquered in more ways than one. She was still playing with the big beads of her necklace. Her long, strong-nailed fingers barely brushed the thin blue line of the vein which ran up from the top of her firm bosom in the thin summer dress. The movement of her thighs was supple and rhythmic as she walked on, carefree and lively, a headstrong mare, a sea-flower blooming in a hot wave.

The tempest blows unleashed. The source of its scorching breaths is the ignition of the pyre within; a fruitless, unabating fire.

She was looking straight at me with her slightly-bulging eyes. She floated in the water which was all around us, clear and blue. The surface was a distant sky where the sparkle of the sunbeams danced; hard sharp points of light, trembling aloft on the rippling globe of the sky. The skin of her rounded neck was adorned by three fine lines and ringed by a wound from which blood poured to make a red streak in the water's depth. A jagged slash, at once hard-edged and thick.

And all around it, the pure, clear, glittering swell.

Her body when swimming had a calm animal fluidity, as if it had no boundaries. But the solid shell grasped hold of it, gleaming green, and her thighs glowed with sweet darkness in the water. And the round spiral shells with shining backs, bristling with spines, were stuck to her breasts.

We were swimming together in the glittering dimness of the water without constraint or anxiety or tension. We were sinking together. We never reached the bottom.

The faint watery dimness was exciting – as was the feel of her body near me, warm and secret, glimmering plump and brown beneath a sea-green dress of fishnets skimming her knees. The threads of the net were soft and finely woven and drawn tightly over her as she buried her face in my neck. I could not see her but I felt the pressure of her wide full lips.

14

I mauled her with my nails and a sprinkle of blood flowed. And a sprinkle of the nectar of love.

The house of love was long and hot and deep and softly-downed, acrid-smelling, secreted within compliant flesh whose fronds had become moist.

Her intimate scent was sharp and pungent. She was dedicated to pleasure. She was the mistress of the games of a passion whose ecstasy is unmatched. She had wisdom, she had a sure touch; she gave me the marvels of her desire, the pleasures of a passion unknown to men.

Still you are ever-present in my inmost soul.

My dreams rove still about your special beauty. My fancies wreathe about your incarnation, your secret.

Is it true I never saw you, daughter of the sea and the earth? Not once all the long days, the years, the ages? What troubled forms then peopled my nightly dreams? In the clouds of your forming in the darkness and in the light? As if from your love there stems but the trial of eternity; from you also the spectres of the daylight which dog me. That and this passion which will not fade or perish.

The fire of the body's affirmation is the light of truth itself, a blinding, inextinguishable light.

The wine of passion is a lush crystal within a grape whose sweetness diminishes never.

Still I travel the wilderness of passion's billowing swell, I thirst for the salt of affection, I suffer the splendours and perils of longing and desire.

My ship is wrecked, I also. How long can I plunge through these high seas?

Will it be near, my haven, or far off? Will there be a boat, there on the sea-shore, waiting for me, left for me, leaning on its side?

2

Posts of Ancient Wood in the Waves

I remember how formidable this high building was, back when I was small. It is formidable even now.

The marble façade towers above me. Between two soaring granite pillars there is a narrow permanently-locked iron gate.

Faces poke out from the small high windows. They are so old we can hardly tell the difference between the men and the women. They are white, with transparent skin over jutting bones, matted hair and sunken eyes. Unfathomably old, they look as if they are detached from their bony frames; they are devoid of all but that last vestige of animation which drives them still to mumble, cheep and whine, in a language unknown to us, through mouths slit as if by a knife.

We are hurrying past; indeed we are nearly running, tugging Aunt Sara by the hand – Aunt Sara whom I love and who is only a few years my senior. I am chivvying my sisters Aida and Hana along in front of me, together with my cousin Maria. Maria is Aunt Hanuna's daughter and she is black like an African but with fine-drawn features, she has a delicate face . . .

We alighted from the Muharram Bey tram where it turned at Wabur el-Miyya. At the tram-turn there was a little grassy garden behind a wrought-iron fence where huge, bright fauvist roses were always in bloom.

We stood with a handful of people in the deserted spot beneath this building, in the morning's pearly light.

16

The car belonging to the young prince Muhammad Reza Pahlavi passed us. I saw him inside the long black Packard — thick eyebrows, a right-hand parting, and a military uniform with the collar buttoned up even in that summer heat. Princess Fawzia, whom I loved, followed in the next car. She was very near to me, very beautiful with her baby face and her two long plaits, smiling toothily. They were surrounded by thin-wheeled motorcycles ridden by great hulking red-faced men; these were English or perhaps Maltese constables. The motorcycles disappeared around the bend at the bottom of *shari'* Fuad, roaring through the quiet reigning over Shallalat, through the fresh greenness beneath the bushy, sinewy trees.

We went to the beach, taking the flight of iron steps down to the shore. Later I would find the little dragon lying enfolded in the living fronds of the water-moss beneath them. The dragon did not seize me then, when I was in that despair which I wanted to be final despair. I took it in my arms and kept it safe in my bed, and fed it on the fruits of my stars.

We ran to the water. My sisters Aida and Hana and my cousin Maria took off the short sprigged dresses they had been wearing over their bathing costumes. The costumes were long in the leg, with shoulder-straps. The waves hit us with solid spray, great spats of foam which sent us running and laughing back . . .

I would pass this building again on my way back from the Abbasiya Secondary School to see the results of the School Certificate examinations. I was with Hasan Abd el-Fatah el-Maradni and Shawqi el-Daba' and Mustafa Mustafa Mustafa — also known as 'Mustafa cubed' — and we were on our way up to the mound. Long and narrow, the mound was reinforced at the sides by large old paving-stones. Wooden posts buttressed the slope at the point where it overlooked the round mediaeval tower of Bab Shawqi police station.

Our hopes were young; they were still rising, hair streaming, from the sea. I told the others how I was going to study Arabic

17

literature and go to Paris like Rifa'a Rafi' el-Tahtawi. I went to the Faculty of Engineering in the end, ostensibly because my father wanted me to be a famous engineer like Uthman Muharram Pasha, but in fact because at that time the Department of Arabic did not admit Copts.

Together we swore undying friendship. We promised to stick by each other come what may. Then we went our separate ways and never met again. Many years later I passed el-Maradni in *shari'* el-Nabi Danyal. We glanced at each other and I realized from the look in his eyes that he was wondering who I was. For that instant between questioning and denial we hesitated, but we did not greet each other. We did not talk. The moment passed and took with it all the years of my boyhood, all at once, and they will never return.

I was here the previous year as well, this time with my friend George who left school before he got to the final year and who told us he had joined the British Air Force. We had a whole tin of bully beef with us – from the Naafi, he said – which we were eating straight from the tin, washing it down with water from a big tap we had trouble turning, and when we did manage it the water came gushing out in big frothy spurts. It was here, back then, that we met an English sailor in a milk-white cap and bell-bottom trousers. I had a copy of *The Tempest* with me, borrowed from the municipal library. Together we accosted this sailor, half-serious, half-joking, to ask him the meaning of certain Shakespearean words I knew already. We were surprised by his composed, cultured tones, by his knowledge of Shakespeare and literature in general – and by his lack of understanding of our country. He was extremely taken aback, not to say shocked, to learn from me that we Egyptians wanted total independence from the British. Evacuation should take place immediately the war was over, I told him. As for George, he told the sailor that the war was heaven-sent and that he would join in the fighting by any means he could, even though he admired Hitler because he was a follower of Nietzsche.

From under this mound and in front of this building I am borne away in a carriage crowded with my uncles, Yunan and Nathan and Surial on my mother's side, and big black Uncle Magar who was my maternal aunt Hanuna's husband; I am dizzied by the blow of loss, by the sun and the bitter sea-breeze. I am borne along behind another carriage, this one black and drawn by six horses all braided and plumed; the pall is slowly borne outspread before it, and on the roof is the youthful golden angel of Death. And I will go out to this mound after the grave had been carelessly filled in and the big men, tunics hitched to their knees and money in their hands, stand smoking and chatting; I do not know where my father's grave is now. My sister Aida whom I loved was carried from here; from here my sister Louisa was taken to the graveyard of strangers. Forty years later the cars came crowding up, horns loud and urgent, behind my mother's funeral procession. From beneath this mound I too shall go to my grave, the grave I know that no one will visit, and I shall see those enchanted slopes again though the fresh green has paled and faded and gone from them and the ancient tree-trunks have dried out and fallen to lie black, fibrous and rotten on the ground; though mud-brick walls of obscene ugliness have taken their place along with the dirty whitewash of the police bureau.

The two thick plaits swung across her back. Against the white muslin of her school blouse they made a special music. It was the plaits which had drawn me like a sleepwalker to follow her all the way down beneath the aristocratic trees of *shari'* Sultan Hossein and then along *shari'* Safiya Zaghlul, where she took the tram to Raml.

I followed her on to the tram and bought a ticket to the end of the line. There was a gaggle of four or five girls with her, all in the same uniform of white blouse, black silk tie and navy-blue skirt. They were laughing and chatting in subdued conspiratorial tones, satchels clasped against their girlish breasts. I discovered that they went to Nabawiya Musa school and I

heard them call her by a nickname, 'Susu'. They alighted after
Sidi Gaber leaving her by herself on the tram. Heart pounding,
the blood draining from my face, I moved to the empty seat in
front of her. Very near now, she was a powerful presence. When
she got off at Bacchus I followed her again, knowing by now
that she was aware of me behind her. There was a tangible,
living tension between us there in the near-deserted street
shadowed by the short, thick, ancient trees. Then she came to
a square house, built of stone and single-storeyed, with a vine-
trellis on the roof. The iron railings had a gate for a dusty path
to the door.

She flicked me an angry puzzled glance as she pushed open
the iron gate, but it failed to discourage me.

I went home as happy and light as a bird. I did not realize
that I had walked the length of *shari'* Abu Qir until I suddenly
found myself in Sidi Gaber again, with the strong, damp October breeze filling my breast.

The ritual of going home with her on the tram to Bacchus,
solely to be with her; of walking beside her or a few stops
behind her until the fleeting farewell glance which altered daily
from questioning to curiosity to invitation to acceptance to
reproach to a quiver of aversion to a secret smile playing about
her moist, slightly thin lips: this ritual was perfect. It was an
end in itself.

I was in love, in the way I usually was when young – and
now that I am old as well. It was a repressed love; I did not
know what to do with it, nor what it would do with me.
Norice Fakhry was my classmate at college and at the same
time a dream which exploded in secret to destroy my soul.
Susu lured me enchanting, and so I risked the adventure. What
could I lose from such love? The whole matter seems rather
amusing now, as if it has shed some of the pain and hurt. But
the pain is remorseless for others just as it is for oneself, it is an
egotistical pain . . .

I alighted from the tram after her. She looked briefly at me.

A light spotty drizzle was falling through the bland golden limpidity of the afternoon light. The sun was wan but it was visible, surrounded by a faint reddish halo.

She hurried out from the shelter of the station roof – an English-style roof with red tiles speedily darkening from the wet. She hesitated for a minute before risking the dash across the street. The tarmac had begun to shine in the light rain.

Without thinking even for an instant I found myself beside her. My voice sounded hoarse and faint to my ears, as if it were not part of me, although the words themselves were familiar through repetition.

'Susu,' I said. 'I want to see you.'

It was as if we had known each other for a long time.

She did not reply. Instead she scrutinized me as I mumbled on with no idea of what I would say next, as if I myself were surprised at what I was saying. 'Listen. I'm at the Faculty of Engineering, in the first year. I want to talk to you about some questions of vital importance. I'll wait for you on Thursday at five o'clock, after school, at the sea-side café at el-Shatbi. Inside. I'll wait for you – don't forget. Five o'clock.'

I did not linger. I turned round, unable to feel my legs carrying me, and boarded the tram we had both alighted from a moment before. I could not believe what had happened. Had I said all that – though it was really so little – to her? Or was it simply a scrap of my uninterrupted train of thought? Was it actually 1943, or did the whole episode take place during some dark and inscrutable escapade of my imagination?

On the dim threshold of the cloudy fantasies of the body I have whispered the secret name. Repairing to the swoon of sins and dreams, I am washed unprovisioned onto the shore of unbelief. My heart has nowhere to live, which is how it is with the hearts of those who are heading for death.

I sent to you – how many times did I send you this! – the salute of the fallen from the abyss of unending silence, and so do I still, so do I still.

The walls of pain are shaking, the beams within as brittle as dry straw. My fingers expire upon a fence tumbling over the mouth of the sepulchre of all things.

His breaths play over my face, weary, patient, wakeful. His eyes are black.

The sea is a corpse cast by the dusk at the city's feet.

The name falls from my lips, in spite of me, into the hands of death.

Did I ever hear your resurrecting voice?

Did I ever see ecstasy's lone star above my roof?

But she came.

The unbelievable, the inconceivable took place.

She was there at the appointed time – in fact she had come a bit early, it seemed. I found her, quiet as a bird, in the round entrance-hall of the sea-side café. The hall was new, spacious and empty, and slightly warm in the early October afternoon. The glass panes surrounded us on all sides, each one tinted a faint pale blue, each one reflecting its own slightly-distorted sea. Between the fabric curtains tied separately to every window the ripples of the coloured blue played with the sea-swell, bending it so that there was a multiplicity of curved, trapped seas . . .

The faces of the dead waved to me with their disembodied hands from the high slits in the marble façade, but I swallowed my fear with the childish forbearance I had not yet lost, and did not scream. Instead I clasped my mother's hand tightly as she walked swiftly and gracefully past the Greek Old People's Home which looked so deserted, where desolation beat at the walls.

We were going to swim at el-Shatbi. Wednesday was ladies' day at the sea-baths.

We crossed the wooden bridge. It was supported by rusty iron pillars embedded in chunks of stone and cement which were buried in the sand. I felt the bridge sway beneath us and looked up at my mother. Her body, in her long soft cream dress, blocked out part of the texture of the blue sky above me.

She gave the money to a woman who was sitting at a table with a little metal cash-box at her side. The woman was extremely fat with frizzy hair and a grotesque face. My mother left her leather handbag with her for safekeeping. The material bag containing an egg sandwich, a hard-cheese sandwich, a bottle of Sa'd Mustafa fizzy drink, a bottle-opener, a comb and a towel – this bag she kept with her. She took a big funny shaped key from a board beside the cash box which had numbers – Western numerals only – on it. Then we set off down between two rows of cabins which were close-set like stalls. All the doors were closed. When we reached the end she poked the key into a long slit and cleverly waggled it so that the door opened with a little creak.

'Wait here,' she told me. 'And don't you budge.'

She shut herself in. Feeling that I couldn't so much as stir, I stood there hardly moving a muscle, awkward and uneasy on my own among the cabins. Then a lady appeared at the end of the passage. She had a wet red leather cap on her head and she was wearing a shiny black bathing-dress which clung to her curves and held her in so that the ample folds didn't bulge out. From that distance I had the impression she was looking disapprovingly and suspiciously at me, but she did not speak. The blood rushed to my face. Then – thank goodness – she went silently into her cabin.

My mother opened the door. She was in the navy-blue bathing-dress she had made herself. It went right up to her neck and down over the roundness of her belly and the tops of her legs. I thought that her body was serene and beautiful, and shining white even though she had caught a little summer sun.

'Come here,' she said. She returned to the cabin and shut the door on us both. The light inside was dim and clear and a trapped watery smell filled the thick air. The wooden floor was slippery, the corners dark with a very faint sharp-smelling sticky greenness. The cracks between the floorboards were long straight slits of light, and from below there came the murmur and slap of the waves.

A long bench ran from one wall of the cabin to the other, the slats dry and clean-looking. My mother sat down on it to pull down my black velvet shorts while I took off my white silk shirt, and off came my loose vest at the same time. She was holding on to me with her other hand so that I would not slip. Then she tugged off my white shoes with the thick grey cork heels, and peeled the white socks from my feet. Her cream dress was hanging on the wooden hook. I watched it billow a little and shine in the pure half-light of early morning.

My mother put my shoes next to hers on the long seat. My shirt, shoes and socks she had folded carefully and stowed in the now-bulging fabric bag; she must have put her clothes inside as well. Then she propped the bag against the wooden wall under the square window, a single shutter which was tough to open and close, overlooking the sea towards Selsela.

Barefoot, panting, I took care not to slip over on the wet floor. My breath had been snatched away by the glee, the novelty of it. We were nearly at the sea now.

We descended the slippery flight of steps to the water. I could see the steps black and distorted beneath the surface and I clutched the handrail. The floor of the sea-side café was over our heads now; we were in the water directly beneath it, close to the sea-bed. Now I was standing on the last step. My red woollen swimming costume, knitted for me by Aunt Sara, was wet. The water was just past my waist and I could feel it lapping, cold and calm, all around me.

The thick wooden posts, reinforced on one side by flat iron struts, supported the café-floor, the baths and the bridge. The water slapped idly between them. Thick ropes stretched trembling from one post to the next, only slightly slack, well above the surface of the water. The water-moss, soft and gleaming

24

green, covered the submerged parts of the posts of ancient wood. Where it rose above the surface it was sprinkled only by the odd slap of foam and quickly dried out. The waves in this watery gaol beneath the café were thick and dark green and gave off a slight rotten odour of seaweed and water-moss, the same as the smell in the cabin. Chilly beams of light were reflected upwards, dancing and quivering, on to the wooden roof above us. I could see the sun's strong glare beating down beyond the edge of the café on to the vast, shifting expanse of open water where the breakers rushed foaming and frothing shorewards, solid masses of water which crashed against the first wooden post to flood gently in towards us, calm and sombre, their spirit broken.

There were only women in the sea around me, climbing down the steps, shrieking from the shock of the water, pausing for a minute to grab the strong ropes strung between the posts and then wading vigorously out into the sea to throw themselves into the tide's free-running turbulence and swim off to a world beyond my reach.

'Stay here,' said my mother. 'I'll be back.'

She left me and launched herself into the open sea, striking through the water with steadfast and experienced arms, smoothly rising and falling with the waves. I stood alone, half underwater and half in cold air, in the sheltered world beneath the café, and it was as if she had left me for ever. I paddled the water with one hand – I had begun to shiver a bit – and gazed at the tall female forms around me. The submerged parts of their bodies could be seen, slightly-distorted, more brightly lit and ripely round in the calm swell than in the air above. My eyes were drawn irresistibly to the shadowy place, plump and mysteriously compelling, between their bared thighs as if I wanted to know it utterly and absolutely. The women threw cautious, kind and perhaps slightly vexed glances at this small lone boy-child quaking from the shock of the sea, the discovery, the strangeness of it all.

Then she came to me. Her long hair was coiled and twisted into a blue kerchief which was still dry. She looked at me with kindly eyes.

'Cold?' she asked, bending down. Her greenish eyes were filled by turns with a yellow light and a hazel darkness as the water tumbled meekly rippling into the clear subterranean, submarine dimness. Her face was a coppery mask, the surface hot in the humid air; it could almost be flat, so slight was the curve. She smiled at me – her teeth stuck out a very little – and lifted me into her arms. Clinging to her large bosom which bobbed above the water I felt weightless. Her rounded back, dark and sturdy and smooth and womanly, was inches from my eyes. My face rested against her long neck and I could smell her special female scent. I was content in her wet embrace; I did not speak; I wasn't embarrassed or missing my mother. I was glad that she hadn't said 'Sweetie' or 'My little lad' – she hadn't even asked me my name. It was as if she knew me.

'Now we're going to swim together,' she said. 'Just pretending, though, not really. I'll hold on to you, love. You wet your head.' There was something sweet and warm about her voice; she had the faintest lisp, I realized, which enchanted me. Without hesitating I ducked my head underwater, and once I had sunk beneath the wavelets I opened my eyes to see a fleeting illuminated nether world, a soundless world with a hidden music. I took a breath and choked, but I loved this drowning sensation and had no desire to surface from it. Perhaps I am still gasping in the same flood-tide. Perhaps I am still searching for a tender affection I want and yet cannot bear.

Between the pillars of the soul veiled by water-moss you are still a single clear star to me. When I fall asleep beneath the damp and flushed face of love my eyes remain wakeful in the thick green rolling deluge. And I have nothing new, not since the heedless days of my youth; I can only reaffirm that which is so certain it needs no reaffirmation; rather my question is endlessly new and my heart is impassioned by the certainty and the question alike.

We left the new café at el-Shatbi – for it was refurbished now – and crossed the stone bridge where a smooth stone wall had been added. We saw the October sun sinking down over the fortress of Qaytbay rearing abruptly and obdurately from the sea. We had told each other about our childhood hopes and failures, and about our dreams whose wild features seemed at the moment of telling to take on a rational, possible, attainable countenance. I told her about my creed in life. I said that Gabra Effendi, the English teacher at the Abbasiya Secondary School, had asked us when we were in the final year what we wanted to be. My friends had said a doctor, a teacher, an engineer, a pilot, but when my turn came I had said 'A poet'. Gabra Effendi had laughed and said, 'Yes, but what else? You want to be a poet, but what do you want to do for a living?' 'I just want to be a poet,' I had replied. Gabra Effendi had not laughed – and neither did she. Instead she told me about her many brothers and sisters, her father who died when she was a child, and her mother who was like a rock, who ruled the entire household with a firm hand. She swore on the Holy Quran that she had never gone out in this fashion with anyone – except her brothers, of course – and that on the Prophet's life she could not think what had made her say Yes, for she had never done anything like this before. She wasn't excusing herself. There was nothing ingratiating about her tone, or flirtatious or condescending. She was simply stating the facts, and although she did not mean it I felt the pain of the blow. But we were happy together after a fashion; we forgot the world as we tend to do in the sunset of our childhood, when we plumb the deepest reaches of the *naïveté* of youth. I had not asked her her name – even now I do not know it. I just called her 'Susu'.

'Let's walk down on the sand for a while,' I said.

Although I had started to get to know her I was slightly surprised at the way she agreed without objecting or even hesitating, and I loved her then, for that alone, very much. She had taken off the black silk ribbon she wore at her collar and her young, fresh, girlish neck looked strong and well-planted on her shoulders. Her low-heeled school shoes did not sink very far into the sand. The wall of the Corniche rose high above us on the right as we walked towards Camp Shizar. The empty beach huts lay beneath it. Each one was different from the others in shape and design, an individual fantasy in the form of a tower or a palace with awnings of straw matting and windows of thick coloured glass. Square or oblong, flat-roofed and low on the ground or high up with two or three steps to the door, they were all deserted. The wood, bleached pale by the summer sun, was holed like lace or plain and scored by thin vertical cracks. Shouts and whistles came from the Corniche above; a gang of street kids had spotted us, but we hardly acknowledged them and they went peacefully past. Although I was momentarily overcome by embarrassment she did not seem the slightest bit concerned. I had been bending down to the sand from time to time as we walked along the shoreline to pick up shells for her – by now I had a little heap of them, shining white mother-of-pearl, rippled red-brown ones, and little perfectly-round spirals which still harboured bewildered, palpitating jelly-like creatures within their deep recesses.

There was a stiff breeze blowing off the sea. Dark clouds were rushing in from the horizon and soon the sky was lowering. Suddenly it turned deep black. The lightning flashed once, alarmingly, through the sunset light, and the wind grew stronger. Violent peals of thunder rumbled directly over our heads as if the world were tumbling down on us, and before we could move heavy fat drops of rain started to teem down. We were drenched in an instant. I could feel the dark firm sand underfoot lose its crispness. Her luxuriant dark hair was soaked at once and fell in dark shining locks over her rounded forehead and down her back. The white muslin blouse clung to her chest. As the wind changed I heard the soft noise of the material as it filled with wind at the front and clung in turn to her back.

With one mind we ran silently to the first beach hut. The wooden verandah was covered and spacious, and the dry refuge felt like the object of a long yearning quest in this downpour which was pounding in great showers on the roof. The straw matting hanging on either side of the verandah and shaking in the wind had begun to give off the sharp, countrified smell of old dry reeds when they get wet. Through the continual gusts of wind I could hear the rustle of the matting as it flapped back and forth.

We looked at one another. Suddenly, without a word, we both burst into laughter.

It gripped us both, this unexplained fit of mirth – unexplained save perhaps by physical ecstasy, by the challenge of youth itself with its strapping limbs. We could not say anything, we were so convulsed. In the clamour of the rain and the wind against the wooden walls our laughter had a pure, near-soundless resonance, yet the whole world echoed with it.

And then I suddenly stopped laughing. Her breasts were firm and pert, her muslin blouse no longer white; it had become transparent and moulded her body, running tightly over her rounded breasts to outline them damply. It was clear to my eyes that they had no support; they were rising freely on their own, unhindered and unsheltered. Her two small nipples were round hardened fruits. Her waist was very slim, as if the navy blue skirt had suddenly become looser. I could see the top of her undervest; it had the pale silvery colour of slightly faded satin. There was a strip of lace, frayed and torn, but the fine stitching joining it to the vest made it look as if it had been expensive and elegant once.

My long blue wool jacket was only wet at the shoulders. I took it off and wordlessly wrapped it around her. She stopped laughing. She became serious and self-possessed.

29

The cloudburst stopped as suddenly as it began. The sky cleared and the sunset light returned, a pallid yellowing gold.

She turned to me and for the first time she asked me my name. There on the covered echoing verandah I told her, and my unmistakably Coptic name sounded odd even to my ears – odd and somehow unjustifiable, as it has all my life. Has it been so, in another way, with my whole existence? She said nothing. Her expression did not change. It was still a coppery mask shining with longing and frustration, a mask with a fresh bloom to it.

Silently we left the beach-house, joining the Corniche at Camp Shizar. I walked with her to the station. When the Bacchus tram came she took off the jacket and gave it back to me without a word, without thanks but also without reproach. She boarded the tram on her own.

I never saw her again.

What did you take away with you, wise little girl, from the adventures of this battered and reckless heart which used to wince at its own pain, which together with you followed a story which had to be cut short?

You are still with me in your single form, your multiplied form, in all the green plains of imagination or the fabled meadows of poetry or the watered places of the spirit, or the spirit's purified deserts, or the peaks of its proud mountains with their spiny crags and I will never visit them all, not ever. You are with me on the shores of the tranquil blue lakes in countries not of this world; you are with me in every fortress and citadel and palace and forest that I will never see.

I came abruptly to my senses. Sand was heaped in my hands. The winter dawn was stealing in through the cracks in the sky. Through a window filled with deceptively mild light a bat shot into my room. An unbearable tautness of wingbeats – and then it settled and was still. Folding its wings it rested there, looking

30

at me with hot bulging eyes which spoke of pain, upon a pile of old dusty books in the right-hand corner of the room. It roosted quietly, a faded, silver, very tangible presence, premonitory yet seemingly invisible, bringing me a message I could never read however hard I tried. It was as if my whole life had come to a halt just before I deciphered the code and now I would never be able to solve it. I was like a sleeper and yet every tremor of my body and soul was fiercely awake. The little dragon was at my side. I could feel its body against me, wakeful and open-eyed. The bat flew from beside the wet face of the old man who stood surrounded by trees, leaving as it had entered, with a lightning flit, with an arrow's traverse.

And I also have no wine left. Only the last lees glimmers in secret but it blazes warmly even so, it will never sink or set. Gall is fixed in my eyes. Passion's founts are waterless. The sky remains shattered against the walls.

Tragedy is not a word.

No, it is not a word.

She will not reply, not even when she says 'Yes'.

Will the living clay ever dry, the clay kneaded with love and pain?

3

Fresh Milk for Half a Piastre

His body besieged him on all sides but there was no escape from the boundlessness marking his bounds, bursting forth endlessly.

He had grown weary of this metaphor which had no possible ending. Nauseated by the minutiae of minutes, by their shadowy light. He sought to eclipse the light and attain a blindness utterly blazing but he knew that he could not do it, that he would never manage it save through the ardour of passion, the craving of the body.

The secret gloom was a fast enclosure and his pleasure was contained therein. In his arms she was freedom and oblivion, her inner fragrance a purely sensual acrid delirium. The silvery satin had a soft nap; aglow with incarnate femininity it brushed his lips and draped fluidly over his face. Her moist eyes were a cruel shining yellow and all tenderness had drained from them to leave only an urgent demand. Her breasts cleaved together, fertility in ferment, belying the slim hollow of her waist. His hand lay on this deep rounded plump tenderness. Wafts of hot-milk aroma came first, a presage of heavy cream, and then a sound as of purling water filled the world and engendered an obscure yearning in his bones; and it seemed his very bones dissolved with a sudden sob to herald the end of this tension, this tide without ebb.

His body still watched over him. A frame possessed but firm and unshaking. Swarms of little black-bodied angels overran him with their teeth, innumerable, bent on the object of their desire; slowly into the hollows of his body they moved, innumerable, their transparent wings white-edged in the sun and fluttering over him on all sides. Their buzzing all around him made all his limbs and organs shudder. He was racked by the almost insensible tickling, by convulsions whose successive tremors ran the length of his limbs in an unbroken rippling. Thus goaded, his skin could not bear the sudden stab tasting of scorching honey, doughy and ripe; his scream was muffled as he was buried between two cloud-banks pouring down rain, a bird with great beating wings swooping down on him to enfold him in its soaked plumes.

Last night we stayed up at celebrate Epiphany. My mother killed a goose. Rafla Effendi, my cousin who was a schoolteacher at the Morqosia Secondary School, came to have supper with us. We put lighted candles inside hollowed and re-folded globes of orange-peel so that they glowed with a flickering light and the pimples on the peel appeared to be made of some brittle and translucent gemstone. My mother had filled every earthenware jar and glass jug with plain tap-water and scented it with incense, because on the eve of Epiphany water left to stand in the jar becomes fresh and good. We got a little tipsy on it; it was as sweet as milk, as sweet as wine.

At first light I went down, half asleep, out of our house on *shari'* No. 12 which overlooked the tram turn at the end of *shari'* Nakhil. As soon as I closed the door I gasped from the shock of the cold air. The noise of the tram scraping on the rails in the square was very loud in the stillness.

I ran from opposite the old dilapidated house at the top of *shari'* el-Ban. The narrow cul-de-sac was still wet after the rain and clogged with mud. I carefully skirted the ruts but my old leather slippers, loose on my feet, were soon soaked. I could feel the muddy water lapping my feet and spattering the hem of my long thick dark winceyette tunic, so I avoided the puddles by walking instead along a narrow dry bank of earth beneath the low stone wall. On the other side was the halva factory, source of the special smell I adored. Finally I reached the high wooden door. In one hand I was holding a big deep copper pan, in my other clenched fist a half-piastre, the kind with a hole drilled in it. I had recently learned to read what was written on it: 'Hossein Kamil – Sultan of Egypt – Five Milliemes'. There was also some writing in Roman script which I could not read, and the number 1335 which seemed magical to me, incomprehensible . . .

My hand was full of half-piastre. I transferred the coin to pan-holding hand, terrified that I would let it slip from my grasp, and reached up on tip-toe to the heavy iron knocker. It was in the shape of a bull's head with an open mouth and horns twisting round backwards. I banged it against the wooden door, once only, far more violently than was necessary.

On the inside of the door there was a latch resting in a slot in the door-jamb. It was attached to a cord so that when the cord was pulled from the inner part of the house the latch was raised. This was how the milkman, Amm Anis the Tunisian, opened the door whenever he was inside in the warmth of his room. All he had to do was call out in his hoarse voice, 'Who is it?', the words strangely muffled by an accent which sounded strange to me; and all I had to do was reply, 'It's me – I want half a piastre's worth of fresh milk' – and without any further ado he would call from within, 'Come in! Come on in, son!' as if I were hanging back.

I leaned my whole side against the door and pushed against it with difficulty. Then I stepped into a wide roofless entrance-hall. It had a dirt floor and there was a composty smell in the air even though there was sky above my head, clear and blue with tiny white-feathered clouds rushing across it.

A thick stone wall separated this area from the bedroom. Three buffalo stood against the wall, tethered by the hind leg with a short thick rope to iron rings set into the stone.

Their dark warm-looking hides were taut over their staring

barrel-ribs and their hip-bones jutted out. They looked at me with their dreadful bulging eyes as they chewed the cud and drooled a gluey white froth from the corners of their mouths.

Amm Anis's donkey, a dainty dandified white one, stood under a sloping canvas canopy stretched over a frame of stout wooden posts and thin cross-pieces which trembled a little.

The thick animal smell was exciting.

The fresh dung under the buffaloes was hot-looking, soft, reeking of fertility.

At the far end of the muddy dirt-floored entrance hall I could see the lad, Saleh. He was curled up asleep, clad in a shirt stiff with dried dirt, on his blanket by the wall. His dark brawny legs were splayed and the bulge between them was large and plain to see. Saleh was short, squat, sturdy and a bit simple. He milked the buaffaloes, rubbed them down and fed them. He cleaned up underneath them and spread out the dung to dry it and make it into fuel-cakes. Every chance he got he kissed Amm Anis's hand, and with Amm Anis's new bride he came and went as he pleased. I was not afraid of him – in fact I liked him. Sometimes he secretly gave me a hunk of hot bread spread with fresh cream.

One of the buffaloes gave a violent snort, the steam coming white from her nostrils and swiftly dispersing. I almost slipped over on a patch of mud mixed with sticky dung. I took myself off smartly to the right and entered the house itself. The bedroom lay at the near end of a roofed and tiled passageway and the door was open.

Amm Anis was sitting on a tuffet making his coffee at the small stone hearth he had built against the high stone wall. The warm spacious bedroom was the only room in the house. I glanced at the big bed in the middle of which, hardly visible amongst the sheets, lay little Amina, the new bride, asleep.

Amm Anis was in his creamy white Tunisian gown. Three or four years later, when we moved to the house by the Mahmudiya Canal in *shari'* Nakhil, the one opposite the stables, he would pass by mounted on his grey donkey and wearing a big hooded

Tunisian burnous over his gown. The burnous was white with a hint of pale yellow and the pointed hood slipped back over his crown as he called up 'Milk! Milk, God's people!' He had grown his hoary beard by this time and pulled it straight and trimmed it. The skin of his face had become so transparent that I could almost see the fine blue veins beneath, but he had filled out and he was a bit sunburned. I had found out by then that his young wife had left him because she had been 'up to no good' and that now she was called 'Creamy Mimi' − but I didn't know exactly what all that meant. I assumed of course that it had to do with the thrilling and fearful mysteries of women. But he had not divorced her; in fact I heard that she had gone to prison for him even though she had already left him by then, and that she had been in prison for three years and all the while he had supported her and her decrepit father and many brothers. My mother said that he was a soft touch, but my father held that he was a decent sort and a gentleman.

Today's prices for Upper-Egyptian wheat sold at the port, Upper Egyptian *foul*-beans, sorted, or grown on the Nile's ebb or on the flood; for raspberries and Fayyumi sorghum, yellow Indian corn, maize, sorghum from Beheira, seed-corn and curved sorghum and fine Indian corn; for whole lentils from Esna and Farshut; grits from Assyut and straw from the Upper Egypt my wily lady love we shall live locked in an embrace and die in a single kiss − if that proves to be our fate − on our way to our own willowy castle, and let us perish in this search for what does it matter if one contemplates as long as the other loves? 'Away! Away! For I will fly to thee not charioted by Bacchus and his pards but on the viewless wings of Poesy! Away with thee! tender is the night, and haply the Queen Moon is on her throne clustered around by all her starry Fays' Eyes burning, filled with fire, towards the frowning shades they struggle in madness, they unite in order to become a single alien and perfect god. 'I received your letter yesterday and was

36

glad to hear that all my dear sons are well. As for us, from Monday until today nothing has happened at all here, no sirens, raids or bombs whatsoever, and we are hopeful that this situation will continue on account of the alliance between Germany and Russia — so we're earning our bread in Alexandria . . .' My beautiful little doll! Who has life for me the way you have life? White, blue, inanimateness living; an ancient temple on a dusty grey mountain; Despair sports with me I feel the cold of his fingers broken in wasted human dignity the notes of a lark piercing the stillness, tresses atumble like night or like sea where darknesses billow, the cure is a sickness and they are the cure, the wise man's fortune the voice of blood shrieked from the depths of a dim silence their bodies are a warm and deliquescent silver. Where are you? She has thrown a diaphanous gilded veil over her clear complexion; reaching deep into dark waterless ravines bristling with meek lily-of-the-valley and wandering songs with neither beginning nor end the evil spirits harry the intimate of passion and ardour; they have swept me away like the scream of a bird in an unknown wilderness, plaintively echoing, and the tenebrous reaches were stilled and the stars paid heed and the flowers were gay: the mad and merciless tempest blew, the horizon quaked, the clouds of the sky tumbled down; the hurricane burst forth with a roar like the cackle of Satan 'But in embalmed darkness guess each sweet wherewith the seasonable month endows the grass the thicket and the pastoral eglantine fast-fading violets . . . for many a time I have been half in love with easeful Death, called him soft names in many a mused rhyme' and as if by the feet of an incubus the flowers have been trampled and the willow-trees lain down on the brink of the brook for the tyrannous wind has torn them down, and the pitchy gloom thickened like a monk standing clothed in coldness under cover of the sweeping branches the tiger waits hungry hidden stock-still the forest in the black of night has the darkness of the desert my heart is an angry colossus of mighty violence attired in a gown of velvety red-saffron and

then my scream resounds deep, ringing, drawn-out, answered
by a thousand mouths, a thousand mocking cackles break out
in its wake, infernal, strange and terrifying 'Eating flesh and
riding flesh and the entering of flesh into flesh' and my eyes
rolled in near insanity as I broke into a run, as an eye gazed in
the late afternoon melting with the waves the toothbrush tree
the iced wine as if perdition were at my heels I went shouting
and stumbling over rocks, colliding with ghosts and knocking
into tombs, my feet cut and bleeding from thorns and bones; I
was on one side of the sides of one cavern of the caverns of
the underworld of the Inferno 'And she in her seat eats a bull
and shits a cow' We received your communication today and
upon receipt of the goods we will endeavour to dispose of them
to your advantage: onions produce of Shandawil, Sohag, Bardis,
Abu Shusha, Tahta, Tima, Deirut, Umeirat, Beni Mazar and
Maghagha, fertilized eggs from Upper Egypt, rejects, and now
for the sales yesterday in the foreign markets: the hundredweight
is equal to 41 okka in the markets of Liverpool, Hull, London
and Trieste − from the daily trade report 'Thou still-unravished
bride of quietness thou foster-child of silence and slow time
sylvan historian who canst thus express a flowery tale' It is love
which appears like a drowsy child grave-eyed and fraught with
longing; how her eyes are like the waves at dusk or wine poured
out by Shahrazad: indeed my heart contracts at the roses in her
cheeks and the whisper of the stars expiring with yearning the
charm of her glance magic runs from her mouth Prospero
the magician of the tempest 'ye elves of hills, brooks, standing
lakes and groves' the sprites who lured Neptune with their
enchanting grace and quarrelled over him 'Oh Egypt this
banner of the Pyramids on the Nile unfurled since the dawn
of Time, over which have marched the armies of Time' and
drowned him 'and ye that on the sand with printless foot' 5
milliemes for milk, 3 milliemes for vinegar, 2 milliemes for
transport from Ragheb Pasha to Gheit el-Enab, 2 milliemes
for the tap washers, 5 milliemes for bread, 17 milliemes for oil,

5 milliemes for tomatoes, 10 for cucumber Caliban the ignoble tyrant Ariel spying the ship's sails as the wind filled them the outpourings of my heart and the droplets of my spirit I have spilled out on to the page my salvation and my consolation there glimmers in my black and desolate life, 3 milliemes for *foul*-beans, 5 milliemes for myrrh seeds, 57 milliemes that is fifty-seven milliemes on 16 March 1942 the prices of onion sacking and medium-weight cotton for gunny-sacks square and oblong ones his thirsty spirit had soared away and left him a body abandoned in sluggish daze, the flowers sighed in their wilting verdure and the gods paid heed and the shepherd boy's tears fell as his only loyal love, his lyre slipped from his hand, who alone had embraced him until the end a light but soon it wanes dearest to my soul you, girl, bringing butter merrily in your jug-jug-jug hey nonny hey languidly glancing they kindle my heart with their languor and the hot coals flow in my tears and so on O deep river valley where perches the cavern of darkness where smiles the temple of dreams O river-valley where the small waves slap in the depths of the benighted chasm and their murmur grows louder; the fresh rose sings upon her swaying bough and the sweet fragrance embraces her in love forge out of your heart melodies linked together like the eternal river Kawthar of Paradise the phrases sung To Hell with To Hell with and thrice to Hell.

'Come in, lad,' said Amm Anis. 'Come in, little lad. Say "In the Name of God" and come in.'

He called from where he sat waiting for the coffee to boil: 'Amina! Come and pour the lad half a piastre's worth of milk, and add a bit extra.'

Then he gave a hoarse belly-laugh. 'Come on inside, then,' he repeated. 'Don't be shy!'

In spite of its size and its high ceiling the room was cluttered and fuggy-smelling. Stacked along one high wall were rows of black cylindrical milk-buckets next to sacks of fodder and *foul-*beans, straw and empty canvas gunny-sacks as well as fabric-covered tuffets laden with mysterious piles of clothes. There was also a big wardrobe, both doors slightly open, dim beams of light glimmering from the interior mirror.

Amina got down off the high bed which rumpled with a froth of piled-up snow-white sheets. Her skin was dark and blooming but it appeared pale at the neck of her silvery-waxen nightgown. The neckline was low and edged with rippling borders of the same colour. The domes of her breasts nestled together; in my eyes they felt tender and firm at the same time.

When she reached the floor, which was covered with a long deep-pile rug from Assyut, and introduced her feet into high-heeled ladies' mules the same colour as her nightgown, I suddenly remembered that she was a new bride. I guessed that she was perhaps the same age as my aunt Sara who was only a few years older than me, for she had a girlish face and her movements were lively. She threw a long shawl of the same colour around her shoulders. Under the tight shiny gown her belly was slender, almost flat, and her extremely fine waist swelled abruptly into full heavy-looking buttocks. 'A Hellenic, Alexandrian urn,' I would say later. 'A real daughter of the country.'

She looked at me, her smile girlishly shy, womanisly seductive. Her short frizzy coarse-looking hair was gathered into an old soft kerchief. I saw that her eyes were wide open.

'Good morning my sweet!' she said. 'Oh, heavens, look at your feet! Completely soaked! Take your slippers off and put them beside the fire – I'll get them dry straight away. Wipe those little toes of yours on the rug. Don't worry! Goodness, if you caught cold! What would your mother do with us? Mercy me, the thought of it!'

I did not reply, but I silently obeyed. I could feel that my face was hot, my bare feet damp.

Suddenly she drew me to her and kissed me on the cheek, squeezing me tightly and tenderly. For a moment I was smothered in her embrace. I closed my eyes and the female smell, that smell which came from sleeping with men and which I knew from the beds of my mother and aunts when they got up: that smell, mingled with the smell of fresh creamy milk, filled me up. Her breast was the height of the upper half of my face, and I felt the soft underpart directly against my mouth. A fleeting moment, a soft split-second ravishment – and then she released me.

With the ghost of an enigmatic smile she dipped the measuring-jug into a large round bucket half-full of milk. It was black on the outside but the inner wall was clean shining silver. She tipped the milk into the deep copper pan with a satisfying sloosh as if it came from a swollen udder. Her kind yellow-green eyes fell soothingly and peacefully on me. 'Goodness,' she said. 'You're shy of Creamy Mimi. But I'm a sister to you! And how is your father? Such a kind, charming man. Do tell him that Mimi says hello. Don't forget, sweetie. Don't let me down, will you. But wait a bit before you go – perhaps your feet aren't warm yet. Go and see Amm Anis – I can see he wants you.'

And she patted my cheek with a hand which felt soft, smooth – liquid, even.

Amm Anis was still seated, leaning back against a slightly grubby bolster. He took the first sip of his Turkish coffee. The frothy surface was dark and thick, and along with the aroma of fresh coffee I could smell the added seasonings of cardamom and North African spices. Without looking down he slipped his hand under the tuffet and drew out a little packet, a piece of white buttered greaseproof paper carefully folded around a small dark firm lump of paste. He bid me hold on to it tight, not to drop it, and to give it to my father as soon as I got home. I often saw my father put a little black pellet like this one under his tongue and slowly suck it with his coffee every morning.

Amm Anis closed his eyes. He seemed to have left us. I went

41

out into the tiled passage where it was rather cold, out into the world, into 'words with neither form nor articulation nor resemblance to the tone of any other sound . . .'

I plunged deep into the chasms of my dreams, deeper by far than I ought: I saw horrors: the goodness of life is the shedding of shyness and though I am young I can do what the old cannot and what do you want of me O deep valley for I surely remember, and the memory is a radiance penetrating a vast darkness a huge open grave in which bones and corpses are scattered and where I stumble screaming 'Where is beauty?' The scent of roses wafts from cheeks oh maidens of poetry and magic bring me a flower who has also lost her way for she has grown to spread perfume and poison amidst the skulls and in the twinkling of an eye I heard a voice from within me: Awaken, man, for you have visited the cavern of darkness and the valley of lights: and yet you were only in the boundless tracts of your human heart, and your path has been in the pursuit of love. So the strayer accompanies the strayer, the wanderer stoops over the wanderer and my heart is swayed *tam tam bar-tam bar-bar tam* a saint with twisted mouth *ba-arawram* 'Beauty is Truth, Truth, Beauty: that is all ye know on Earth and all ye need to know' is that not so? Almighty God Your mercy is divine divine: do You not hear me? Are You not moved by the shriek of a rending heart? Can You not pardon the errant sinner? For You are boundless mercy You are complete and untainted Love, Lord, hearken unto me Almighty God take my hand Aphrodite took the bow and the needle and fled the world of darkness and sewed it with silken velvet in the sight of Neptune who plunged into billows of soaring spume and water-moss and in the ocean's depth Aphrodite dyed it with a shining essence of sapphire which stares in the eyes of water-sprites Tear – my God – the veil from my eyes – my God – deliver me from evil have mercy on me Kyrie Eleison Kyrei Eleison oh beloved of

42

men I am but a soul razed smooth by your hands by a sublime wisdom I know not a fire roasting a heart which is ardent, and the light is annihilated under the feet of darkness the wind is cooing and the dew glistening in the spirit's dimness enchantment and peace I shouted in a godlike and tyrannical grief My God, my God, why hast Thou abandoned me, *Eli, Eli, lama sabachthani* have I been given this grace only to grieve over it lips braided with crimson in a sea of blackness the sparkle of your eyes in the shackle's harshness and now I return loaded with my harvest of brittle chaff my bliss lies in my dreams in my ivory tower in my seventy-seven heavens in my seven hundred darknesses and not in that filthy runnel they call life Eros oh unruly child eternity past and future will never overcome the power of your bow and arrow, neither will Death nor Hell 'And about the air-raids; after the one on Gheit el-Enab and Ghurbal I told you about before, we've had only one little raid, last Tuesday at dawn. They bombed the railway – they were aiming for Kom el-Nadura but the bombs fell on the earthenware and china warehouses. About eighty shops were destroyed but the losses were slight – only thirty killed and seven injured – and this was because there were no houses above the shops, and people have started to come back to Alexandria.' Her magical musical voice with its rising and falling notes, her radiant smile, her innocent childishness: in her voice there is an ocean of feelings and unexplored regions God curse these girls laughter a sweet light poem coming unfaltering from a pretty graceful elegant mouth and looks short sweet hidden unfaltering from tranquil eyes freedom raise me to the light of a world of imagination to the exclamation of joy at the slender shapeliness of beautiful women and Su'ad how far away she is and a group of Upper Egyptian bakers in the alley the dim light from an oil lamp in the pitchy night O goddess of eternity since eternity I worship her and with the blood of my heart sacrificed I would ransom her 'and what do you have of her? Just this coupling done by eyes only, though your cock stands up hard' and they laugh and laugh and begin in warmth and solitude and darkness to bet and joke together, voices rough and hoarse, rare strange laughs in which there is a ring of misery and endurance and I have passed the night on my bed a couch of thorns with my heart grieving for a distant distant morning 'O Attic shape! Fair attitude! with brede of marble men and maidens overwrought with forest branches and the trodden weed, Thou, silent form dost tease us out of thought as doth eternity' What is effaced is all a conquered pain appearing from time to time, in a husky shaking voice which is almost slumbering a world desolate and bleak surrounded by oceans of feelings and unexplored regions: Oh my heart sing in praise of a pure wine which is good and the lips are a fire like sweet water, and tell me: can there be an excess of passion? So sing my soul for existence is but a mystery to Hell with to Hell with and thrice to Hell.

Before I was imprisoned on 15 May 1948 I had rented, under an assumed name, a room built on the roof of a four-storey building which was in a street off *shari'* Irfan in Muharram Bey. Things were easier in the forties. It was a quiet side-street shaded by ancient trees. There was an old iron folding bed in the room; it was rusty and the springs sagged, though the mattress itself was good and the sheets which I had bought myself were snow-white. There was also a wardrobe with a loose rickety door, and it was in here that I put the Marxist and Trotskyite books and periodicals I had ordered direct from the publishers. They came from Europe and America, arriving at a PO Box at the General Post Office at Manshiya. I also had the originals of our revolutionary pamphlets and tracts, and the magazines and books we bought from Schwartz Bookshop in *shari'* Safiya Zaghlul: and in addition to these I had piles of translations, hundreds of copies of short stories by Gorky and Chekhov which we produced ourselves, at our own expense, from the translations by Fawzi el-Murr and Shafiq Raqim.

I also put into this wardrobe three Italian hand-grenades left over from the war and a small Biretta I had confiscated, on behalf of the Committee, from Ahmad el-Nems after I had convinced him that individual acts of terrorism were futile. Assassinating influential capitalist exploiters was pointless because they were a class, not a collection of individuals, and that in consequence the collective class 'terrorism' as practised by an alliance of oppressed and exploited classes and groups was the only true democracy. Ahmad was a member of the Muslim Brotherhood in the beginning, but once a Trotskyite he never broke faith, not even after the passing years had turned him firstly into a teacher in the Congo before it became Zaire and then, in Geneva, Paris and Vienna, a freelance translator for the United Nations.

I bought a vase and put flowers in it. The flowers came from a gardener in the district whom I wanted to enlist in the movement. I also collected any thin dry twisted twigs I found on the pavement and trimmed them into special arrangements in which I could see a special beauty. My belief in life then was that Revolution could not dispense with aesthetics. Furthermore the flowers and twigs served as camouflage against the neighbours, who believed that I was a painter or art-lover of some kind. And there was also a primitive Gestetner copying machine, a glass case with a rubber cylinder inside; and there was a sideboard and a lamp.

No chair, no rug, no mat, nothing. It was very bare, but even so it was filled with a spirit of intimacy which was at once very personal and completely impersonal. Nobody knew the address of this room except Qasim Ishaq, the brilliant Nubian prodigy whom I loved and who left our group to join the DMNL – the Democratic Movement for National Liberation – and who died of cancer after spending half his life in jails and internment camps. But I always kept the key with me. I do not know what happened

45

to the precious books, the weapons, the flowers after we were imprisoned – both myself and Qasim.

When I suddenly saw her in *shari'* Irfan I almost spluttered with shock. I had recognized her without a moment's hesitation. Immediately I went over to her. When I shook her hand I found it was flabby in mine, limp and nerveless.

Her blue three-quarter-length jacket hung down over a silky dress which looked dark red in the shadow of the street. It was probably made out of the parachute silk, sold in bulk in the Ladies' Alley, which came from the job-lots of English goods abandoned in the warehouses after the war.

She panted and clung to my arm all the way up the four flights of stairs. I imagined stealthy eyes fixing me from behind the closed doors. The room was very cold in that winter weather. I shut the door behind me – and found her in my arms. The touch of her finely-chiselled lips was soft and warm in the cold; mobile, lively lips. Her trembling abated in my embrace. She put her arm over the side of my face and covered it completely. I could no longer hear anything in the world except the clamour of her body leaning gently against mine.

The lamp light was a gentle glow on one side of the room. It lit up an area of white wall, one corner of the smooth and shining white bed, and the sunflower. The water had dried in the vase and the glowing petals had withered into a hard tenacious stiffness. The rest of the room lay in a secret gloom, the double wooden picture frame on the wall barely discernible. There were two pictures in the frame, cut out from books, and there was no glass. One was Albert Qusayri and the other Leon Trotsky.

My eyes met hers. They were large, pale, very close to mine and just now slightly hollow. There were wrinkles around them, very fine in the smooth dark skin, and it was as if they did not see me because they were enveloping me in their fixed and solid waves. But in my arms she was an inexplicable freedom, an oblivion.

46

I had come out of prison after a two-year stretch. Now only the last batch of internees was still inside. My friends who had worked for the cause had grown older and had lost their enthusiasm for the acts of insurgency they had undertaken in their youth. They avoided me until they were convinced that I too had despaired of it all. I didn't even read *al-Ahram* any more.

Raml station seemed to belong to another country, one I did not know and in which I knew no one. The imperial palm-trees were barren, two opposing rows of tall elegant flaxen-plaited trees, strangers to me. And the people whom I had imagined that I loved with the love of Christ and Trotsky combined had passed away into their own lives, their own diversions and seriousnesses, into the town tram and the Raml tram, far, far away.

After prison my engineering diploma was a burden. I did not know how I would manage to support myself, my mother and my sisters. I gave up taking the tram and when I walked, lonely and troubled, to Raml station each afternoon I did not buy so much as a thirteen-millieme bottle of pop on the way. I didn't have enough in my pocket for that. My philosophical cynicism, my poetical bitterness over all of this was intolerable. What was the meaning of this deprivation? Why was it import-ant? But in spite of the childishness of this speculation it was, even so, extremely depressing.

So I concealed the fact that I had a diploma. As I knew a couple of words of English and French I finally managed to get a job as a 'workshop assistant' with a Franco-Egyptian building company in order to earn ten pounds a month, which was fortune indeed since Egyptian engineers were not the objects of welcome and acceptance, not even by companies in 1950. After that I moved my family, my possessions and my love from Raghib Pasha to Cleopatra; for as soon as I had begun working with that company I had fallen thunderstruck in love with my Ni'ma, my steadfast rock. But even so my despair was total; of life, love, politics and poetry.

47

In the morning, half-asleep after sitting up late with Mallarmé, when I was in the bus which followed the shore and stopped in front of the Cecil Hotel, where I changed for the bus to Dikheila – it was then that I saw the tanks, armoured cars and troop carriers clattering along the Corniche. The noise was whipped away by the sea breeze so that they seemed to have nothing to do with the city or the people living there. They were heading towards Ras el-Tin, it was not clear why. It did not look serious or threatening to me; they gave no cause for alarm. The waves at el-Mina el-Sharqiya looked artificially blue as they beat against the big crooked slabs of cement hidden underwater there. The edges broke the surface by the wall of the Corniche but there was no surf. The few people around, some barefoot in long tunics, others in short-sleeved shirts or complete summer suits – they all stopped for a moment. Some of them called out unenthusiastically for God to bring victory to the Egyptian army. There it was: the most important event in our recent history, happening before my eyes without my taking the least account of it. Or understanding what it meant.

I was not then nor am I now very far from you, you restive little boy tormented by the tearing of your body as your raw stuff was rent and remoulded into its final form.

I see you now in the middle of a clear Alexandrian night at the beginning of autumn. The moon is round and made of solid silver, annihilating the sky with a brilliance which electrifies your skin. You are in the ground-floor drawing-room which looks out on to *shari'* Ibn Zahar. The set of wooden chairs, upholstered in blue sprigged fabric with a grey nap, was still new and strong, and loomed large in the moonlit room. The ground-floor window was two tall panes above a horizontal stone ledge. Where were your parents, your sisters? Had Death the prowler snatched any one of them away yet? Were they sleeping, in inner rooms closed upon their sleep? It was as if the flat which overlooked *shari'* Raghib Pasha on one side, not far from *haret* el-Gullanar, was wholly yours, utterly and absolutely yours.

You had been struck by your first true love, that love which would remain buried and unspoken; and the blow had struck you deep, deeper than anything you had known from your boyish loves, your translations of Shelley and Keats, your tears for the Arab poets exiled to America, for Marguerite Gautier, for Anna Karenina and the sufferings of Werther, and the poems of that naïve and melancholy spirit; all your wanderings in words, the wilderness of words.

That small copper pan your mother used to fetch the Nile perch from el-Mallaha. Scales silvery-shining, smooth, an innocent clean fishy whiff to its freshness – this pan is dry now. Papers are piled up in it, crumpled and torn; bills from your father's business which failed years before, the gaps on the paper filled up with poetry; shiny paper from school jotters covered in minute writing; light, faded white rice-paper covered with words words words; thick paper with a sharp crease which had a dry woody rustle, covered all over with a dialogue between Christian angels and Greek gods, romantic sprites and naiads which you had never seen but which crowded that nocturnal strand.

A drop of gasoline. A match. All along the length of the window open to the empty night the flames of a little blaze can be seen, dancing, pale yellow-white, in the flooding light of the moon.

There is a smell of burning paper. The billowing smoke pours quickly out into the street and disappears. The smoke from a lock of short black curly hair is thickly acrid, penetratingly greasy. The scorching of an ignited scrap of fabric from which an ancient and intimate dew has dried, clung about with living fancies, reminds you of the spitting of the stove, the hidden fire spreading through the thorny scrub of the cemetery.

When the immolation of youth was about to be complete, your heart disobeyed you.

Fine tongues of flame burned your fingers as you rescued a black-bordered scrap incensed by fire, scorched by it at both edges.

The smoke of that desperate blaze is lifted up to whom?

Who will receive it? Will it seem good in His eyes?

Or will He refuse it and return it to the boy crossing the threshold into manhood, whose steps stand still in Time, who will never ever set down his feet?

4

The Silent Madonna of Ghobrial

I was accompanied every morning, on my journey from *haret* el-Gullanar to the Abbasiya Secondary School, by two dreams:
the cinema
and the Madonna.

At exactly five to seven, by the clock hanging in the hall, I went out.

I had folded a double sheet of *al-Basir* newspaper around my textbooks and novels so that my sweaty hands would not stain them. I hardly felt the weight of the *tarboosh* on my head. The cold damp air was blowing in on my chest through the open neck of my shirt, the sky aglow with the wide virgin daybreak. At the fork in the road, where the black tarmac gleamed after a hosing-down or a passing spell of drizzle – here, on the façade of the building confronting me at the junction, was the thin wooden frame and raw primary colours of the billboard of the Roxy Cinema.

And then there opened the gate of my dream.

The greatest love story the steed a pure blue and pitch-black prancing on its hind legs the enchantress of the Southern Seas I hear its coloured neighing as I astride it unsheathe the red sword and brandish it skywards with a heartless smile you are my prince indeed the domain of your excellence knows no strife and to whom can I say as my ancient forebears said, 'Recollection has withered me'? The temptress with parted thighs with breasts two perfect hemispheres bluish beneath Qais's charger which is attacking and retreating at the same time and the chestnut steed of Ibn Abi Rabi'a which did not reveal his secret even though he stammered it out in her red veil outspread over the ocean's shore beneath the marble of the green-braided imperial palms the adventures of the knight conqueror of heroes sharp Toledo sword of Indian steel and wide eyes shafting me Layla al-'Amiriya, Sappho, Virginie, Thais, Greta Garbo, Hind – would she had kept the promises she made to us, Gloria Swanson, Mona, Maria the Alexandrian, Magdalene, Azza the beloved of Kuthayir, Marguerite Gautier, Ginger Rogers, Rahma, Loretta Young, Creamy Mimi, Behiga Hafiz, Judy Garland, Linda, and the owner of the blue silk robe in Muharram Bey who cares why do rebellious tears forestall me, why am I assailed over and over by the mournful strains of that bygone and ever-present time? I kneel down beside her on the sands of faraway islands between equatorial breakers the obscenity of her parted and encarmined lips is irresistible and my arms are beneath the sunken yellow cloven belly and Arabic and English letters overspread what is above her thighs with empty spaces between them attraction in its final week due to public demand.

And in the afternoon I ran to the old newspaper vendor who lent me magazines for two and a half milliemes at a time, *al-Hilal* and *al-Muqtataf* and *al-Magalla al-Gedida*, and paperback novels as well. He had his wares spread out on the pavement in front of the Electricity Company building in *shari'* Salah el-Din. Then I would walk rapidly past the cinema opposite the tobacconists at the junction of *shari'* Raghib Pasha and *shari'* el-Khedive Tawfiq. An antiquated wooden warehouse with a flat tin roof, the gate of the dream, prison-like, where an iron grille came down to close off the darkened hall. I never once went in.

All the fruits of dreams so close so dear I did not pick all the whinnying supernatural steeds I did not mount all the gentle pliant women to whom in the tenderness of their sex I will never make love all the seas into whose billows I will never plunge their whirlwinds did not blow me nor did the parrots cackle in their jungles all the prisons of dreams whose locks did not surrender to me and the heavenly spheres I wished to embrace and clasp in my arms all the marmoreal palaces of the Thousand Nights and their wave-beaten caverns all the ghouls and whales and monsters and Cyclopses and houris with sealed pudenda and the murderous infidel jinn-women and the speaking apes and the birds with long red beaks and leather pouches loaded with emeralds and sapphires praising the name of God all the majesties which will never come to be: and can we ever return to the lost places of boyhood and youth resurrected from their deep grave Alexandria of the thirties, Cairo of the fifties, the St Petersburg of Dostoevsky, Akhmim of the forties, the Paris of de Maupassant, the Moscow of Chekhov, the prairies of Gogol, the London of Dickens and Thackeray and the Lakes of Wordsworth and the mystic gardens in the Bengal of Tagore: and returning is a constant delirium and there will never be a return.

Suffering is easy and somewhat trite. But this is not, of course, the case with tragedy.

Why this tarrying by the ruin's detritus? This is the habit of your ancient forbears, circling a shrine that God had forsaken never to return.

'Now' for you is an expired and bygone day. You have no 'Now'. That which has died is in continual resurrection from Simeon's tomb, it is a kingdom which will surely come.

All that has passed away. It is dead.

Do you not wish to be content? Will you never desist from falling by the traces of former encampments?

Do you not know how to conclude the rites of farewell?

53

The stuff of dreams is fragile and wispy. It binds my wrists and ankles, as unbending as iron bands.

The boy had not yet encountered the mature man, his adversary and twin who knows now how ferociously he fought to fashion a superabundant life crowded with achievements, who let 'real' things slip unmourned through his fingers, wealth, power, women. Still he seems not to realize that he has passed through life as if in a dream, that he is on the periphery of life, that he is a man of desire desiring what does not exist . . . so he said.

Why do I find that the sloping potters' yard in Ghobrial is always dim in the first light of morning – dim and unreal? Why do I see it, spacious though it is, as if it were entirely underground? Where is the clarity of the brilliant morning sky, the white clouds? There seems to be a roof above me, made of canvas, a few scant drops of light trickling through – canvas, or heavy gathering clouds.

I passed behind the Evangelical Church along a narrow paved passage between two very close-set buildings, to find myself all of a sudden on the threshold of the wide potters' yard. From there I travelled down over the bumpy ground pounded hard by many feet to a twisting alley which led me out on to a broad tarmacked street overlooked by the lush verdant slopes of the Abbasiya Secondary School hill. This threading short-cut gave me over twenty extra minutes with my schoolmates before the first lesson. But the most important, the essential, the fundamental thing, was that just as I came down to the sloping yard, as I slipped past the big kiln which was permanently alight with a suppressed scorching flame – exactly at that spot, on the summit of the world, at the same time to the dot every day, I encountered the Madonna.

She shone, my lady whose light lit up the drabness of life. She came out suddenly, at exactly her appointed time, from the single side-alley on my right. As if she had descended from Heaven to me alone.

The first part of the potters' yard contained shops. In the glow from the yellow-flamed gas lamp I could see a lot of bare wooden shelves inside, not a thing on them, and the closed wooden doors of the kilns. They were made of planks knocked together with huge nails into a single piece, and the fire blazed, pale in the morning light, through the cracks. And there was a legless beggar who looked as if he were guarding the kilns, apparently stuck by the hip-bones on to a flat wheeled board which he pushed along as if he were also hammered on with stout nails. Every day at that time he would be eating *foul*-beans with oil and cumin from a deep tin dish with a bit of what could have been sow-thistle or rocket and a toasted round of yesterday's bread on a newspaper in front of him. There was another beggar with him, a tall dark-faced man who used to come up the stairs of our building years before in Gheit el-Enab and stand outside our door – the self-same man, half-naked then and knocking a stone with a dull thud against the staring ribs of his chest. I heard his hoarse choked voice: 'My supper is in your hands oh Lord. Whoever brings good in his hands will find it. For God's sake, O charitable people.' I ran to mother for her to give me a big toasted piece of flat bread for alms. He took it from me – I felt his strong-boned fingers – and tossed it into a bulging sack, filled to the middle with bread, on his back. He looked scary back then, very close to me; seemingly from another world, it was true, but I feel truly that I came from him and that I shall end in him.

The Madonna appeared suddenly and my vision of things fled away. There was only her.

The Virgin Lady, bringer of light, Sitt Demiana, Santa Katarina all at once.

Who was she?

Why did it concern me? And why did I care what she did in life, who she was, what her relationships, what her circumstances, whether she was a teacher at the primary school attached to the Anglican Church where my sister Louisa studied? I did not ask her. Was she a salesgirl in a department store? Did she work at the mill with Mona's sister Gamalat? Was she married or not? But I knew that she was neither single nor married, she was beyond that, she was not subject to the laws of this earth.

The fire of her eyes in mine, just for an instant. The shadow of a faint illusory smile, almost imperceptible. Every day. Every morning.

I was aware only of that which is beyond bliss, beyond sensation.

And then I went up the hill to the Abbasiya Secondary School amongst the crowds of schoolchildren who were also climbing the long tarmac path which wound its way upwards to the big schoolyard. I was walking in step to my own private soaring music.

Still I see her face, faintly tinged with rose, finely sprinkled with tiny scarcely distinguishable spots, her pursed lips a deep crimson. And the feel of her face: oily, greasy, soaking into the dark rising dough of time and glowing with it − even now it permeates my night and entices my limbs, even now it is my icon from the church of Abu Saifain in Akhmim, from Raphael, Pinturicchio, Da Vinci, Coreggio together. It is gone from the earth but not forgotten, it is a lasting immanence. Her eyes which are a lake with wide-flung borders, golden-green − these are the eyes which shaft the boy and man at once with agony, with enduring passion while pillowing him in snug content.

Silent Madonna of Ghobrial.

Her body is an altar, her legs two strong smooth draped columns with one secret and treasured capital. Baptismal font and source of the water of life from which I drink and never thirst. Her breasts dazzle as if blessed, suckling the world on the milk of human kindness, rounded beneath the hand-knitted pullover which was red one day and blue the next, turn and turn about without a break – all year she wore the same clothes, except at the beginning of the summer before the holidays when she put on a silky cream-coloured blouse. As for her skirt, it was always black, invariably black, an unfading unchanging unalterable black; very long, black wool or summery floaty but always a pitch, a jet black.

On the right of the slope as I went down there was a large dusty square with stacks of pottery arranged in rows. Tall terracotta jars, pitchers, jugs, tall beakers, flowerpots, shallow dishes, bowls for milk and yoghurt, charcoal braziers and ceramic stoves. Big, small, straight-sided or bulging, the rough texture of the clay scratched my hands, smooth granules like invisible pin-pricks, as I awaited the grace of her manifestation. The big kiln in the shop at the end with the narrow door – I could feel the blaze of the fire within it, flaring away pent-up inside, burning with an incessant agitated hiss. The potters stood all around the door, in the kiln-room and in the square, small and black, vigorous and gaunt-faced, knobby knees bare beneath short, sleeveless shifts. They wore skull-caps, dirty white or dark red felt, wide turbans with the loose ends showing, and tasselled scarves. They bent over the fire or slept exhausted or bought and sold like sultans, but I never saw one of them at his wheel. Did they bring the raw clay from its distant mysterious places? The very stuff of their lives? Where were they in the dimness of the morning which daily veils her face in clear water – whose eyes close in a smile of death which is in itself life in completeness, pure and secret content, peace entire?

They had pulled her out of the water at el-Shatbi the previous year, moments after she had vanished beneath the surface, eyes closed, smiling. From that same spot they would bring out the body of the German pilot with the Iron Cross still on his chest though the fish had eaten away his face and nibbled his belly. The smell was a mixture of corruption, disintegration, excrement hanging in his gut, and interior gangrene – intolerable.

57

The waves beat on the land of my nightly dreams repeated through youth and into middle age. The dust of the potters' yard, the alleys ascending to it, leading down from it, twisting and narrowing between long long walls of unfired mud-brick, turning their backs to me. Narrow doors open on to darkened hallways where women hunker clad in black peasant gowns with gathered yokes but the doors suddenly and soundlessly swing shut in my face and the walls are once more blank without breach or aperture. They close in on me as I run borne on the wind, effortlessly, and then find myself crawling on my hands and knees through a tunnel in the earth, the odour of old dust filling my lungs until I ascend to the surface and come down on to the traitorous earth which plunges down with me. What is chasing me? Who pursues me with such determination? I cannot see him, I do not know him. I feel only his panting breath, his unflagging intent. The beggar, the legless trunk of a man, guffaws soundlessly in my face, the monkey-man holds the little monkey as if it were his foetal son, his withered twin, he drags him by the neck on a thin chain I can feel it pressing on my neck, I gasp for breath. On my right and left they rise up, in front of me and behind, a closing circle of them, stacks of jars and jugs and tall pitchers leaping up to surround me, to menace me, to topple – I am never aware of them falling, they seem always on the brink of smashing down. I return unexpectedly to this earth where waves seem to beat on its borders from beneath, invisible in the labyrinths of the night. The wandering is repeated night after night but it is a desolate land. The Madonna has left it and passed on. I wish to liberate myself from her but am not delivered.

Smooth hands with long tapering fingers. Ivory nails the colour and sheen of mother-of-pearl. A hand closed to grasp the other raised hand; she pauses to touch it tenderly, to embrace it in a final moment of repose. And the hands together hide the face in which alone was my salvation beneath a white

58

semi-transparent semi-opaque veil, a thick yet diaphanous watery mist.

After the summer holidays I did not see her at all. I never bade her farewell.

She is still with me, living under my skin. She does not want to absolve me.

I leave this land suddenly to find myself beneath this high hillside green with plants unknown to me. My mother holds onto my hand tight and I feel myself dwindling as I cling to the black shawl wound tightly round her body. Surrounding me there is a band of women in shawls, gowns, peasant scarves. Tall figures jostling together in the breathless crush, they move slowly, solidly, inexorably towards a little door where a stout man in a grubby white coat is standing. He is holding the door nearly closed so that the women have to go in one by one, each with her son or daughter, shutting it forcefully after each entrant, planting his legs firmly on the ground so as not to fall over.

My mother was taking me to 'the Englishwoman' for her to examine and treat my painfully red eyes. I remember the sharp point of the long silvery-shining needle piercing my eye, my scream of ultimate terror as my mother held my arm and hugged me tight. I remember the tall shining nurse enclosing my face firmly with her hands to keep my head still so that I couldn't move or flinch while the skinny stick of a doctor, her clear icy-blue eyes trained on me in firm kindness, introduced the needle into my eye with her wafer-thin hands. The overwhelming panic from that moment of shock is still with me today.

'Lady Cromer Clinic'. I read the sign now, the Arabic and the English above it, on my way to the hill I was to learn was Abbasiya Hill. I see the same door, closed now, the street clean and deserted in front of the long low wall overhung by the thick leafy branches of trees. There are mysterious buildings

59

behind the trees, pointed roofs made of dark red clay tiles, tall high-set windows criss-crossed with iron bars.

'Lift your head brother for the age of colonialism has passed.' The deep magical voice which had for so long intoxicated millions and filled their breasts with elation. 'Colonialism has lifted its staff on to its shoulders and departed never to return.' Would that it were so! How many times have we lifted our heads, and how many times have we bowed them again. Soldiers are still standing by closed doors, doors shut fast, to beat us with thick staves and thick leather whips which descend on the bones of the back and shoulders to crush them like iron.

In the house in the district of Cleopatra Hammamat, before going to my book and bed, well after midnight, I would stand out on the rather small balcony filling my lungs with the faint salty tang of the night air and looking at the trees below me in the garden of the houses opposite, across the sleeping street. The strip of sky between the rows of roofs was silvery, or pure blue, or running with the great beating wings of cloud-birds.

That night I heard the middle door, the one next to mine, stealthily and noiselessly open.

And when I stealthily and noiselessly looked through the inch-wide chink in my door I saw Paola the Italian woman standing outside her family's bedroom. Her loose plunging pink nightdress hung by thin straps from her broad rounded shoulders.

She stood still. I could feel that she was tense, reining in the vehemence of her unruly body as she stood there in the dim glow of the five-candle-power night lamp. Beneath the lamp the six high-backed chairs and the long dining-table, the cloth removed now by my mother, loomed through the half-light.

She stood by the door as if she were looking inside herself, as if she saw nothing of the exterior world. Immersed in the light's mournful pallor she was extraordinarily still; she was letting herself sink for ever downwards in it without arriving at the bottom.

I knew that Antonio, her strapping young husband, and her daughter Carla who was about my sister's age, were both asleep in the one big bed.

My father had been dead for many years by now. We were making ends meet by renting a room, sometimes two, in our house over the summer, by the week, the month or the whole season according to circumstance.

At that time I had a job as a workshop assistant at the Franco-Egyptian company Battignolles which was constructing the harbour at Dikheila. I would leave the house at exactly five to seven every morning – I might have had two or three hours' sleep after staying up to read American novels and French poetry. I had long ago abandoned my revolutionary political work by this time – along with my revolutionary puritanism. I had learned how to get drunk, to smoke like a chimney, to stay up late at Friscador Cafe after roaming the streets – and other places – until past midnight. I loved my enduring Ni'ma with a piercing, tormented, devastated love, all the while taking Odette to the cinema or to Pastroudis Café without doing more than occasionally holding her hand in the darkness of the film and kissing her cheek upon meeting or saying 'Till next time!', sometimes, and never promising her anything more than that, not under any circumstance.

Was Paola about forty? She had a youthful ebullient body that summer; she seemed to attack me with her abundant femininity. In the morning she came to breakfast with her bosom almost bare beneath a thin billowing blouse which, as it drooped down over her full breasts, echoed the soft thick fall of her hair tumbling loose over the jut of her shoulders.

She was Alexandrian, originally from el-Attarin, but she had married Antonio who owned a garage and mechanic's workshop for cars in the quarter of el-Zahir in Cairo. She had gone to Cairo with him when they got married years ago.

And during the evenings she would open her door and say flirtatiously to me 'Buona sera – come 'stai? Esta' bene?' – her eyes alluring, the green a deep blue, the shallows dangerous and slippery.

'What is this! Always with a book in your hand, my dear! Even at mealtimes. Day and night, day and night. Don't you ever feel like a bit of the *dolce vita*? A little walk along the promenade? A bit of singing and dancing?'

In a completely Egyptian accent, the accent of a real local girl. Well, almost.

Antonio was born in Sakakini and went to the Don Bosco School. He was a brawny man whose shirt was always open to reveal thick black chest hair. His forearms were muscular beneath short sleeves which clung to upper arms bulging with virility.

As for Carla, her fine-boned virgin girl-child's body was all sharp angles, restless movements, fiery eyes. She was darker than the Egyptian girls; no one would guess that she was Italian.

Paola was a Sophia Loren or Claudia Cardinale type. Warm and Egyptian-blooded, she plunged into life with sharp wits and a sunny nature. There was an experienced look about her body; it had an easy-going but at the same time impregnable air. She seemed to foreshadow, to presage some part of what my voracious jinn-woman, the priestess of my dragon, my Manat, my lily of the valley, my Nun, would turn out to be.

The smoothness of her face a secret guarded since the beginning of time, marred nay perfected by tiny near-invisible pocks: a softness seemingly occuring beyond the body, beyond ecstasy, beyond time. A perfection of existence with neither beginning nor end. The hot white bodily mist ascends, soaring and twisting in sharp-tongued scraps with a continual insistant hiss sensual delicacies draped in the folds of passion the threads of love embrace the tenderness of that abundant rounded belly and pull tight with a sudden tearing of the cloth as if it is burning with an invisible fire and the noise of warp and weft parting is an unexpected whisper and the passions lie prostrate, sagging and spent on the open shore the death-groan in lust and ardour and passion an agony whose pleasure is unending and my devoted heart lies spent before the pale of breasts charged, teeming, pouring forth and drenched with a pellucid veil of dew a slow ascension to soft pastureland and the gongs resound without ever swelling to the tonguing of great bell-globes but the bell's belly vibrates and swings high heading unmoving for a clangour which fills heaven with mighty echoes to the furthest corners of creation ropes hanging the length of the lofty tower and stretched tight by desperate hands around the waist of the last the ultimate the thunderous bell, upright and unrelenting solidity surrounded and enfolded by the darkness of the flesh of love the ore of this earth a blazing silver and gold, wood and iron, glass and copper and the essence of plants smelted within a subterranean passage to flow and sink thickly in heavy ignition indriven by all-conquering power extinction touches it not.

I came home late, after the cinema and a final cappuccino at Friscador Café, to find the main hall of the house in uproar.

My mother was calm, her eyes shining with resolution. There was an idea fixed unshakeably in her head. She was speaking to Antonio.

'Listen, sir,' she was saying. 'Here – take the rest of your account. You can leave the house tomorrow. Be so good as to oblige me. I can't do without my son!'

Antonio's reply was so tempestuous, he was almost bellowing. He put two fingers to his head in an unmistakable gesture. 'I . . . I . . . it's a fine thing when you come out with . . . this! My wife is a gem, she is as white as snow, as fresh milk! Now I'm just a local boy, a bit footloose, I know. I've been around – I've been with Alexandrian girls from Anfushi to Abu Qir but they all left me cold . . . and you come to tell me about your son? You come and speak against my wife? With . . . *whom?* That's a fine thing! Shame on you, madam. By God, shame on you, madam!'

'Don't you madam me, sir! This is my final word. Tomorrow by sundown at the latest. Things have gone far enough, sir!'

Paola was still standing in the same place, by the door of the middle room. She said nothing; she stood bare-throated in her plunging blouse, her heavy breasts motionless.

As for me, I was dumbfounded. I did not speak. I had grasped the entire situation. I could imagine what had been said and I could not bear the thought of what had been said. I divined the secret knowledge which was passing wordlessly between my mother and Paola; no one could have refuted that intimation. I opened the door and went silently outside again, leaving her to gaze unspeaking at the entire scene like someone entertained by it, or someone keeping quiet about something which had not happened at all but even so could never be disclosed. As if her husband were a cross child left too long alone with his toys. But her understanding of what my mother was doing was alert and fully conscious even though she would deny it, she would not admit to anything under any circumstances.

That night I walked along the calm and fast-emptying Corniche. I walked nearly as far as Ra's el-Tin and missed the last tram. I came back by taxi in the small hours.

Paola did not exonerate me either.

I went back to the prison camp at Abu Qir. Barbed wire, and beyond it the vast rolling dunes rising and falling all the way to the distant buildings. Guards slouching in wooden huts at the top of high watch-towers, thin-barrelled machine-guns slung from their shoulders – far away but definitely, categorically, forbiddingly there.

I held her hand in my hands, the soft fall of her hair in my hands; her head has no body, her head has been gently detached to lie alone on my chest, eyes closed, lips barely parted in an enigmatic and endless smile.

I saw the apes aloft like airborne monks, cloaks flying in the wind as they swam through the air just as they did in a film I saw years later starring Omar Sharif and Sophia Loren. The apes were leaning out through windows which had been cut out of the walls to glide alone on the wind. The square frames were made of new, untreated, unseasoned, unpainted wood. The apes were female, buxom, medium height, their clothes flimsy and elegant, tight skirts and silk blouses cut low to show the cleavage of their proud domed breasts. Everything about them was alluringly feminine − save their faces, which were in featureless darkness. How did I know they were apes? It was the dumbness. They were not capable of speech. Not a murmur, not the slightest sound could they produce. They were silent. They flew beyond windowpanes flying in the blue.

My father
once said
There is a spell I know which the ancient Egyptians wrote, and it is buried now beneath Pompey's Pillar but the passing of years does not thwart or weaken its power. A talisman which prevents the kites, the eagles and vultures and all birds of prey from swooping down out of the Alexandrian sky onto the victims beneath. Instead they keep wheeling and soaring, they cannot come down. However much they struggle against the spell's hold its magic is stronger. And the female apes with voices stopped up could not alight.

I loved with a love akin to madness.

My window is open and high. Sunny in the afternoon. Suspended in a wall which the sea has broken through, a wall penetrated by the clouds of the sky. White gulls, black gulls stand on the shoreline in the glittering shallows, in the calm, rippling, salty blaze.

And I tell you that one evening you will go, the one ever single and multiplied, ever ancient and renewed, and I will forget, I will forget the whiplash scoring the living flesh, the scream of death. Hot water trickling bores hollows in the granite of an immovable column which is shaking now. When will it fall? The water's obdurate descent, the gasp at the dream which grips my bones to smash them, wear them away, change my body utterly. The water of night will trickle away, the dark incubus lift from my breast. The hard pebbles of my heart are unsmoothed by the waves of the years which break unrelentingly on to the ever-parched and treacherous sands. Will this fissure close? Will the stab-wounds of ancient passion ever be healed and not bleed afresh? The ruins of the spirit collapse without a sound?

I will forget the flash of light in your eyes.

When?

When will dusk fall, and the disc of the sun sink into the sea?

5

Bullets and the Passions of the Clinging Vine

On the Corniche at the far end of Rushdi Pasha there is a stone stairway – I can feel it now under my feet – carved out of basalt and leading down to the first part of Stanley beach.

To my left on the way down, the little square in front of the Rushdi Café which is always empty even in high summer. To my right a high wide wall, blank and captivating, with no window or aperture of any kind. A cream-coloured wall, grown over and clung about with the ramified sinuosities of a flourishing dark green creeper.

Suddenly I find myself swiftly climbing these rocky steps.

Suddenly I find that they are very big. They soar bumpily upwards, rough to the touch, their sharp edges closing in on me from all sides. The rocks have become vaster, more menacing and more perilous as I rise. Now I am not looking down or behind. I continue to climb these huge cloud-roaming crags. The sea lies far, far below.

I cannot go down. My feet refuse to move. I stand stockstill, seized by the fear that I will trip and tumble head over heels, tearing my limbs on these towering jagged murderous steps.

And yet why do I fear? There is no need to be afraid. I know that this is a dream.

I am really awake. I simply haven't opened my eyes yet.

Go down, then.

I can't. No – I *am* in a dream. The dream is controlling me. I am in the grip of the dream.

Even so, the fear prevents me from believing that it is a dream. If I am in a dream, then I'm done for.

I am outside the dream. Nevertheless I am beset by uneasiness.

I say: It isn't far. It isn't so very high. I shall go down.

You will slip. You will fall. You will die.

It's no distance at all. Nothing will happen.

No. You will come to grief. You will arrive at the bottom a corpse.

I cannot wake up from the dream, but I know that I am outside the dream.

Wake up now. Go down. Truly you have come out of the night.

No. You will remain for ever in this dream.

I shall cling on to the rocks. I shall hold fast. I shall not fall.

No. You will never awaken, not unless you go down first.

Abruptly my feet betray me and I really do stumble. I fall through the air, I crash against the rocks, I roll over the jutting edge which hurtle up to hit me and pass by as I plummet on downwards. Not one echo do I hear of this scream which is filling heaven and earth.

On my right the wall stood upright, secure and immovable. The vine's branches scaled and embraced it like a soft verdant carving, plump at the base and then thinning and narrowing out to hug the wall in an almost translucent network.

Built to a multi-layered architectural design, the villa enclosed by this leafy wall was a luxurious well-tended dwelling on a gentle slope. It had a view of the Corniche on one side and the sea on the other. The garden was bushy with trees, rich with a variety of plants; if I stood on tiptoe on the first step of the basalt staircase I could see into it. I wanted to jump down over the stone wall and simply stand for a moment in the clean tiled inner courtyard where the autumn leaves – and each individual leaf had its own being – had fallen on to the white tiles. Crushed pale gold crumbs of yellow casuarina leaves scattered across the smooth gleam of the marble, Christ's thorn and olive trees, and a lone regal palm, springing skywards in utter grace from a wrought-iron ring-fence bounding the rich clay at the bole.

I knew that this villa – which was like a bashful jewel even so – belonged to Rodolphe Mitri who was in our class at the Abbasiya Secondary School. He wasn't a friend of mine. Wealth either inherited or acquired left – and still leaves – a sour taste in my mouth. In addition he had completely different concerns in life. The Packard which brought him to school, driven by a chauffeur straight out of the movies in a cap and a jacket with a tight collar and a long row of big buttons. Stories about girls recounted by him in ringing tones every morning before the first lesson, with the boys clustered round drinking it all in. His great number of extremely smart tailored suits, all nipped in at the waist. His ties which were obviously silk, each one of which could have fed my family for a month or more . . . and so on. But we still said 'hello' and exchanged a few words. Everyone in the class knew me well. He couldn't pronounce the letter 'r' and he spoke, like a lot of well-to-do sons, in a carrying but unpompous voice, in a stylish classy manner which was all politeness, which seemed absolutely natural even though it had been dinned into him. I didn't hate this way of talking but I couldn't and still cannot warm to it. Even now when my beloved Rama speaks to me in this fashion I feel an icy shudder constrict my spirit.

Rodolphe was one of a band of pupils known as the 'big boys'. It was we younger nippers who were top of the class. We were all devilry and naughtiness, addicted to studying, mad on reading and high-toned discussions. I can still picture Rodolphe's round, rather flat face, his Douglas Fairbanks moustache, his puffy eyes sluggish with easy living, good food, nights of fun with girls. We knew that he came from a notable family in Assyut, rich Protestant Copts who only came to Alexandria in the summer. Rodolphe passed the rest of the year alone in that smart villa with the cook, the driver and the maid. I remember once we were coming out of school at the end of the academic year – all heat, crowds, hubbub, afternoon humidity, merry goodbyes, arrangements to meet, boys running about. A woman was approaching down the narrow alley in front of the school gate – a fine figure of a woman, her white dress tight across full firm buttocks which alternately rose and fell in time to her deliberate steps. All by itself, the sensuous rhythm had transformed the shabby buildings and lent a definition to the everyday scene. By chance I was next to Rodolphe and none of our classmates was nearby. Suddenly his eyes lit up. He could not help himself.

'Wheew-ee!' he said. 'Take a look at *that!* What an . . . *eyeful!*'

In the days when I thought I was a poet I used to go out on clear winter Friday mornings to Stanley Bay. I feasted my eyes on the tender sprigs of greenery covering the smooth wide wall. I found a romantic missive written there; an intimation of the beauty of Creation itself was borne to me on those quivering tendrils, racking my heart and soothing it at the same time. I went down to the rocky strand, the shore of sand, and there in the salt spray I looked upon the sea's margin and sank into a reverie of small eddies, a fantasy of shallow hollows in nook of rock and hummock of stone where sky dwindled rippling into an imprisoned glitter in level clefts a handsbreadth deep. I observed the attrition of the sea outflung and spent upon the sand in foaming froth and stubborn shushsh, time after time without end. And my fumbled thought was: All this is eternal. It was here fathomless aeons before I saw it. It will remain, fathomless aeons after I am gone.

70

Was I not a poet?!

And in the days when I thought I was a revolutionary, on occasions such as the king's birthday, the run-up to demonstrations, the aftermath of students' or workers' strikes when I knew or suspected that the police were going to raid the house, search it and take me off, along with the usual band, to the main police station or if I were lucky to the gaol for foreigners and 'politicals' – on these occasions I would spend the night in a room rented all year by my friend George at the 'Serene' Hotel overlooking Stanley Bay. No one would ever suspect George of being a political activist.

At night I would descend the basalt steps to watch the convolutions of the creeping vine as it pulsed in the tall street lamp's electric light, possessed of a clutching, malevolent, voracious life of its own, coiled as if to attack. My thoughts however were of the villa. This well-planned comfort was the right of every family. I boiled with pent-up anger over the shabby ugly dwellings we had lived in all our lives, the homes I entered when visiting factory workers in the districts of Maks, Bacchus or Hagar el-Nawatiya in order to instruct them, encourage them, prepare them for action. I yearned with all my rebellious, trembling heart for some form of justice and truth.

And in the days when I was the licit spoil of a love which determined to choke me in its vice, when I was the prey of a despair I imagined to be cosmic metaphysical, absolute, and when the November afternoon skies blazed with a refreshing damp-winded fire which nevertheless appeased me not at all and conveyed to me no meaning at all – then I would drag my heavy limbs down to Stanley Bay to lose myself in dark meditations on the lure of death, on its futility, on all the impossibilities of life. Was it in vain I sought the dragon, my awesome creature with gaping maw and tongue of fire, as if I wished it, as if then I would find some as yet unformed salvation? Or was it seeking me? The branches of the vine clinging about my

71

wall were hot, the growth thick and heavy now, the writhing turns all but blanketing the wall, binding it to couple in unquenchable lust, a body composed of teeming darkness at once impenetrable and inescapable.

And in these last days? Now that I have come to accept, without caring overmuch, that any one thing is the same as the other, that my life has taken its course as chance would have it, good and bad, *naïveté* and foolishness, old gnawing pains and old glowing joys, fragile glories long-gone and ever-present frustrations: only now, after all this, have I come to realize (or think I have come to realize) that love is a delusion, a sensual dream, and the strong shy friendship between men is like all else a mere settling of accounts – and even if they are emotional accounts, my friend, they are still accounts. I thought: I have drunk at the rill the source of all things, and do you think I am quenched? Still I thirst, my lips despite the lengthy draught are parched, they are constantly bitter as aloes. I said: Justice is an old wives' tale, beauty a withered leaf trodden underfoot, art a fruitless vain endeavour and all things, all things are but vanity, fear, hunger and iniquitous chaos.

I said: Rail and slander, then. Throw back all your gifts.

I said: Nobody delights in the body's delight, nobody is intoxicated by the spirit's ecstasy as you are. Therefore why these sorrows?

I said: These are the well-known depressions of old age – and of youth. All true. All unsound to the last.

Then did I discover all of a sudden that the smooth skin of the once-alive, once-organic wall, the soft surface coat, had peeled away. Now it was disfigured by black pocks and abrasions. It has suffered injuries and nobody cared. The vine had become scorched, it had dried up and fallen away, and the unchangingly beautiful villa was derelict. Tattiness and dilapidation had taken hold, and where was Rodolphe Mitri now? And I discoverd all of a sudden that the little café – the one beneath the smart secluded hotel – where Odette and I used sometimes to treat ourselves self-indulgently to a delicious cappuccino for seven piastres (plus two for the waiter) – this café had been transformed into a restaurant typical of the 'open-door' era, an obscenely tawdry place, revoltingly affected and pretentious, showy in the most repellent and artificial manner possible.

This is how it was with the passions of the clinging vine.

They have grown like the vine, my love's passions, in Alexandria my great city, God-preserved harbour, golden haven, vision of Alexander and work of Sostrates the mighty engineer, pearl of Cleopatra the eternal beauty, shining marbled city which at night needs no illumination so white is she; academy of Archimedes, of Eratosthenes the philosopher, of the poets Apollonious and Callimachus, dwelling of all the muses, capital of sanctity and profanity, land of St Mark, St Ananius and the founders of the Bucolic Church, of Origen and Dionysius and St Athenasius who stood prophet-like alone with the truth in the face of all the world; city of Patriarchs, pillar of true orthodoxy, diadem of the seventy thousand who will rise up with shining-white faces at the side of Christ as seraphim in all their glory sing God's praises; Ras Pharos casting its light from green Eleusis el-Hadara to Canope-Abu Qir, from the Gymnasium and the temple of Poseidon to the Emporium and the Stadium, from the Hippodrome to the Serapeum, from the Ratotis mount-Kom el-Shaqafa to Selsela-Loqias Point, from the Panium mount-Kom el-Dekka and Camp Shizar to Petrai-Hagar el-Nawatiya; harbour unmatched save by Calicut, there bursts from her heart the stout obelisk of stature unparalleled on the face of the earth, none so firm so unleaden of limb for it is conjoined in unbreachable union. Pompey's Pillar carved from the marble of Ibrim's mount most finely worked at the crown, girded most skilfully, wrought most craftily – peerless; city of pastures, gaols, schools, theatres, city of columns city of four thousand baths and four thousand clubs all fit for kings four thousand grocers selling greens alone never mind the thousands of other shops; bride of waters pouring from the Red Sea to Gibraltar Straits, community of shrines from Sidi Mursi Abu'l Abbas and Sidi Abu Dardar to Sidi'l Shatbi and Sidi Gaber and Sidi Kireyim God be pleased with them all; city of wide streets and august arched edifices of sure foundation, wondrous of breadth, splendid of habitation, lofty of pride, Alexandria O Alexandria rampant sun of my childhood thirst of my boyhood and beloved of my youth.

I said: Do you still dream of perpetuity, of that which surpasses eternity?

I said: Do you not see that this is an evil dream, that no good will come of it?

I said: No.

Philippe Nakhla was a workshop assistant with me at Battignolles. He was the only person in the company who knew that a long time ago, before I went to prison, I had taken a degree in engineering at Farouq I University and that I had been obliged to conceal this in order to get a job worth ten pounds a month. Gabriel Hawwari, a Syrian-born construction engineer working for Battignolles, had been a fellow-student at the Faculty. We used to laugh at him a bit back then, because of his accent — his family spoke French at home — and his dull plodding ways, but now I kept out of his sight. I avoided him because I thought he had come to discover that I was working in the company solely on the strength of my School Certificate. At the same time I believed that he had somehow agreed to collude in this, and not to give me away to the directors of the French company; and without so much as a word or a look I thanked him for that. He might have found the whole matter rather unimportant, in any case. Or, possibly, he had simply missed me; luckily he worked at Head Office, not on site.

74

Philippe Nakhla was very tall and very thin with a hollow face. His father Tadros Effendi Nakhla was one of the heroes of the 1919 revolution whom the revolution betrayed and whose life hopes were consequently dashed. He spent ten years in prison on a bombing charge. After he was released, on a special dispensation, he was employed by the Wafd government. Then, under Muhammad Mahmud's government, he was given a post in the furthest reaches of Upper Egypt, so he took early retirement instead and worked on the Alexandrian newspaper *al-Basir* as a copy-editor and proof-reader. He married an Alexandrian Greek woman who bore him first Philippe and then Iskandar who later worked in the 'Leadership of the Revolution' building in Gezira and who married a French woman fifteen years his senior. Tadros's wife had died just before the war, leaving him on his own with their two sons. Once, when I went to their ground-floor flat in the large old building next to the Graeco-Roman Museum, Tadros came out into the reception room. It was a huge dark hall with an enormous marble table in the middle covered with a lustrous tasselled cloth in dark green velvet. I was sitting in a daydream on one of the high wooden chairs which were carved in the Art Nouveau style popular in the twenties. As he came in I stood up – and tripped on the faded Persian carpet. The threads at the edge, it seemed, had come loose and frayed. He greeted me with a mortally cold handshake. His eyes, dimmed by letters and trials, stared indifferently through bottle-glass spectacles at a spot just to one side of my face. He was also lean and spare, and he never took off his ancient *tarboosh*, not even when he was wearing a loose robe at home.

Something about me attracted Philippe – all my life there has been something in me which has drawn strange characters and eccentrics to me – and it was we two who became friends, without any ostensible reason, out of all the company employees. He was responsible for checking the Supplies Account for the workshop: lime, sand, cement, reinforcing steel, filling rubble, ceramic tiles and so on. He used to fill in the supply order forms and send them to the operations manager who would check them and prepare the order in the usual way. Not until years afterwards did I learn that Philippe had been playing a clever and undetectable game with the figures. He had collaborated with the lorry-drivers on one hand and the operations manager on the other in smuggling away small quantities of 'supplies' – each consignment worth a trifling amount in itself, but the loss was continual and in the end it added up. The directors, unable to find any evidence at all, could pin nothing on him. Finally they asked Philippe and the operations manager frankly if they would be so kind as to resign. Although I had nothing to do with them apart from my friendship with Philippe, which was a matter of common knowledge in the company, the French manager gave me to understand that he would like me to resign as well. If I did choose to stay he could do nothing about it but, he hinted, my prospects of advancement in the company were nil. I refused to resign then, and I did not leave until six or seven months later. The company gave me a warm letter of recommendation and my next job was that of restorer at the Graeco-Roman Museum.

Philippe spent his money steadily but without extravagance. He told everyone that he was using up the small legacy left him by his mother. He was sunny, talkative in Arabic, French and English, and never sat still for a minute. His deepset eyes twinkled in their bony sockets. He also took out loans at interest and borrowed against his salary. He was in love with a pale Yugoslavian girl called Janine who lived alone with her old mother in a flat in el-Attarin. Years later he worked as a translator at the Indian Embassy at the northern end of Zamalek. I visited him once or twice in his little basement office. Later I learned that he had caught TB and died shortly afterwards.

He used to come to our house in Cleopatra Hammamat – very early on Sunday mornings, waking me up by opening the door to the little balcony overlooking the garden of the old house which lay across the still sleeping street. My mother would make him a big dish of eggs fried in cooking butter from Upper Egypt, and another of *foul*-beans with olive oil, while I made do with a bit of hard cheese and a boiled egg. Then we drank our tea and went out for a walk along the Corniche. We bought fresh lettuce, rinsing it in cold water from the pitcher in the street – the stallholder asked for half a piastre extra for the water. Peeling off the leaves we joked, chatted and laughed and ate it, fresh, crisp and juicy, translucent green and dripping water, as the purifying sea air filled our lungs. Below us the tranquil autumn waves met the sands with a low gentle hiss, the regular rhythm infusing my senses and spirit in a manner hardly perceptible, while the clear morning light of Alexandria shone radiant from the heavens to fill my eyes, and nowhere on earth is there anything like it.

Ah, the mornings, the early mornings of Alexandria.

One evening we went to the 'Serene' Hotel just at the end of Stanley Bay, myself, Philippe, and Thomas Shukri'llah, his Syrian-born friend who was a French speaker like him and who worked at the Eastern Export Company Ltd in Maks.

The usual night-club gloom pervaded the large salon. The music produced by the little orchestra was likewise subdued, almost murky in tone. Small dark-red lamps, like grapes, slowly blinked on and off.

Without preliminary Philippe said 'Did you know? Gabriel Hawwari died this afternoon.'

I did not say 'How?' or 'When?' or 'I only saw him a few days ago – was he ill? Did he have an accident?' I didn't ask any of these questions which have no value, which come simply in the shock of the moment as a weapon against fear. As an attempt to ignore the impossible.

'You've made me sad,' I said.

I felt a hollowness in my heart. As if part of it had been cut out and taken away.

Philippe looked at the girl sitting at the bar not far from us. He smiled at her from under his hook of a nose, a nose like the beak of a mild-tempered scrawny bird, and she came over to us. I moved to make room for her. She sat down between me and Philippe and turned to speak to me. Unsmiling, serious, as if she were about to discuss a matter of some importance. Was it my obvious *naïveté* which had attracted her? My virginity, perhaps?

'What will you get me?' she asked.

'Anything,' I replied, rather mechanically. 'Anything you like.'

'Whisky?'

The headwaiter, a think dark hatchet-faced man, had already approached and was standing nearby. I signalled to him but was pre-empted by Philippe. 'Four double whiskies,' he ordered.

But apart from a bare glance of acknowledgement, swiftly made, the girl paid him not the slightest attention. Still without smiling or flirting or any hint of triteness she said, 'How are you? What are you doing these days?'

She's just making conversation, I said to myself. She's saying anything.

But her voice seemed familiar. A voice from a long time ago, one which nevertheless I could not place.

As she approached me through the hazy gloom I had seen that a very small part of her delicate upper lip had a forward jut to it, and that her lower lip by contrast was plump and drooping, giving a blatant sensual cast to her face. I thought: Am I sure I don't know her? There was a charged quality in her nearness, likewise in her femininity, which was not strange.

I was also startled by a look of pain in her slightly swollen eyes, as if I had hurt her in some way.

And I felt, and denied, that there was a bond of sorts between us, a relationship at once intimate and forgotten.

I told myself that I had never been here before in my life, nor anywhere like it, and that I didn't know any women like her. She glanced away just then as if she had summarily dismissed me. It was absurd, but I was a bit stung by this – I who had been telling myself that of course I didn't know her, that she meant nothing to me.

Philippe, who had been sitting there tensely all the while, tossed his whisky back. 'Let's go,' he said. 'We've been here long enough. I'm bored.'

It seemed that his masculine pride had been hurt by the way she had concentrated on me. Although he had invited her and was obviously paying for the drinks she had hardly noticed he was there; except, that is, for that one moment when she had shunned me in the wake of some small disappointment, the frustration of some expectation or desire.

Thomas Shukri'llah spoke. 'Yes, let's go,' he said in French. 'The French troupe is on tonight.' He winked. He meant those very ungirlish girls, Madame Artur's dancers, who were then performing in Alexandria.

Abruptly she got down off the bar stool beside me. She stood there for a moment, head up, without speaking. She had hardly touched her drink. She walked away, dejected and proud.

I did not remember her.

When towards dawn I got to bed, my head swimming from the late hour, the drink, the unaccustomed adventure, the sensual riot – just as I was on the verge of sleep I woke up with a jerk. I *had* known her! All at once I was back in the small bar in Bab el-Karrasta with the woman who years ago had saved me from falling into the hands of the authorities, perhaps from prison itself, by foiling the plans the detective had laid to entrap me. But try as I might I could not remember her name. The darkness of my room was an oppressive weight. I turned on the light, wide awake now and wretched. I promised myself that I would go and find her the very next day and kiss her hand. I was unable to sleep until what seemed like an aeon of regret and pain had passed. I was falling, wounded, tripping and tumbling over sharp-toothed bumpy rocks. I knew that I was not in a dream.

I did not go to see her the next day. I never saw her again.

I remember her name now, after all this time.

Zizi – that is the only name I know you by – where are you now? Are you still living? Where? How?

The cold wind of the Corniche buffeted us. I turned up the collar of my big navy-blue coat. It was a British Navy mackintosh which I had taken from the depot at Kafr Ashri with the written and officially-stamped permission of Mr Lee the depot supervisor, during the war. I wore it for years and years, through good times and bad. My mother brought it to me after I was interned; I took it with me to the prison camp at Tur and back again to Abu Qir. Finally I abandoned it – almost unwillingly, as if under duress in the light of our long acquaintance – simply because I had got so sick of it that I couldn't bear to wear it any longer. It was still in good condition when I gave it to the Church. I had always prized it and taken affectionate, appreciative care of it.

'Tonight we're going to paint the town red!' I said in English.

We crossed the Corniche, shoulders to the wind storming in from a dark angry sea which was beating against the sand with a powerful insistent rumble.

Now that night had fallen the Scarabee looked like a little fortress with its study round tower on top. A lantern swayed above a wooden door set into the thick stone, a little red light with strong wire netting around the glass.

We were met by a headwaiter in a black tail coat. Philippe passed him something he had been holding in his hand, half-furtively, half-openly. Straightbacked and moving with a confident pompous gait which managed at the same time to convey respect for his guests, the man led us to a round table bordering the dance floor. The show began, in a roll of drums and a noisy but harmonious fanfare, with the famous French can-can. The girls turned their backs and bent over to reveal red-veiled buttocks puffed out with rippling frills of lace. Turning again they kicked their legs in the air, all black fishnets and high stilettos, nearly hitting us in the face. It was a daring manoeuvre, studied and elegant, almost but not quite obscene. Through the dappled dimness their cheeks looked gaunter, hollower and deeper-shadowed, their pert breasts fuller and higher-thrust. In the brief unexpected lulls in the music I heard the muffled rush of the sea beyond the stout walls, the howl of the wind.

In the early afternoons of cloudless winter Sundays I used occasionally to go with Odette to the Scarabee. We sat on the sunny balcony and drank Martini or Campari, alone – or almost alone – with the wide sea's blue, the white foam's gentle hiss.

We were on our fourth or fifth drink when the girl appeared. She was a slender angular sort of creature, very *soignée* and artificial. She sat down beside Philippe.

'My name is Sylvana,' was the first thing she said. 'What's yours, darling?'

I said in English to Thomas Shukri'llah: 'Of course the headwaiter is in on this. It's a conspiracy.'

Thomas stifled a snigger, as if he were trying not to hurt Philippe's feelings.

I repeated it clearly to Philippe in Arabic. 'Lucky man. I didn't know the headwaiter was your uncle. With friends like that, you've got it made!'

Philipe gave a restrained laugh. He had never really learned how to guffaw. I never once heard him roar with mirth.

It was obvious that the girl had not understood. She gave me a sharp, rather vicious glance. 'What did you say, dear?' she asked me in French. Her voice was husky, with a harsh, slightly cracked ring to it.

'I was just saying how chic you are, *ma belle*,' I replied smoothly.

She didn't laugh. She didn't look as though she believed me. She leaned towards Philippe's glass and took an ostentatious flirty sip. The headwaiter materialized in front of us and Philippe ordered another round.

Her dark brown hair was primped and fluffed to fan out over

her sharp shoulders. Her legs, meticulously encased in black stockings, showed long and etiolated beneath a floral silk dress slit at the side. Her bare arms were two pale wands, as if the thinnest of cushioning layers lay between skin and bone; their slenderness was exciting. Her eyes were heavily rimmed with kohl. A wide gold belt encircled her narrow waist, fitting almost as snugly as a bracelet clasp or fettering strap; tugged in as tight, as tight as it could go and yet the loose folds of her dress over her bottom, the vertical breach in the side of the skirt, gave me an impression of openness, of something being offered.

I have a fuddled memory of the feel of her bones after the eighth or ninth drink, her bones hot beneath the cool fall of silk as she grasped my arm on one side and Philippe's on the other. I remember one rather harsh laugh, muffled and whipped away by the wind, coming from Thomas Shukri'llah; and I remember the Corniche rising and falling under my feet in an alcoholic whirl, the cold blasts of dawn wind restoring me as I gulped them in, the steps leading downwards, the long corridor of the Seranada Hotel. The warm glass-fronted room skimming the high winter sea, the big cosy brown bed, the picture of the naked reclining woman whose skin had a sheen like a fish.

The threads of lust tauten and stretch to the last ounce of strength in their fibre, to the farthest tolerable limit of extension, the belt tightens bounding the fragile waist the gold chain swings over the peaked domes of her breasts in the cling of the shiny brassière encumbered with its compliant load the earring dangling from the delicate lobe to tremble a drop of musk from the liver of a slaughtered gazelle the wide bracelets clasp her thin upper arm or her slender waist or both together the shiny strap of the brassière held by fine hooks binds her upper back to grip it to press the spare flesh under her armpits so that it looks soft and blooming and the kohl which serves to emphasize the merciless craving in her eyes, the dark depth, the rapacious glitter the black beauty spot on her taut cheek softly suffused with blood, almost as black as the two heavily pencilled bows above her eyes curving downward in the ancient Alexandrian style of Cleopatra, words of lovecraft stream from her lips, she moans with pleasure at the act of love the smile of the wide mouth the lips suffused and agleam with carmine close about the hot solid column of love and the interior is ablaze and the pound of blood alone is audible, a crashing of bones as once again the creation resounds with the music of the carnal tenderness a rose of the fire of demand, the pangs of anguish burst forth from an obdurate bud cleaving wickedly and the sighing embrace when all this ceases to be the slim belly's whirlpool perfectly round and complete the cup of sweet Arab coffee I sip a scant drop the shackle of burning thirst close rigorous sharp clutch of long gripping nails hands featherfine stroke with gentle skill the lotus incensed with passion a kiss withheld a drop of saliva still barred still forbidden the top of her slender thighs ringed by a garter sprinkled with golden sequins loosely clasp the sheer black stocking the accoutrements of sensual desire soft and slithering beneath the fingers at her neck a scarf tied in a big knot on one side and the scarf drifts unhindered across her naked back falling with deceptive gentleness the narrow buttocks pressed firmly over the locked-in embellishment and wrapped in the taker of the embrace the walls liquefy as if they are open to receive the tumultuous wave of ecstasy with the sound of a crash of waters softly-desiring a fountain cleaving the earth of a pliant smooth body a single body merged in the gown of braided darkness a heavy flow atremble a warm distant wave hotly athirst for imminent consummation and fighting prolongation still it has a flare that impassions my inside who are you behind that open mask? Who are you alive within me I want you unceasingly and however I surround you in my arms in my entirety far out of reach? The edges of the fabric gripped and stretched to the farthest edge of Creation suddenly slipped, split, whirled with a dull explosion into a dance outflung and spent the body's anger the madness which defies futility.

In another crowd of long men's tunics, women's black wrappers: where am I? Squashed and squeezed amongst feet legs sides I cling for dear life to my mother's hand face upturned for air in the midst of the choking crush I catch a bare glimpse of the window criss-crossed by iron bars in a poky sandy yard, breathless female voices piercing and fervent, husky male voices running the words together as they call names and salutes, 'How are you Usta Hossein, how are you my brother. Our Lord lighten your burden!' It was Thursday 21 July 1938, half-past seven in the morning Western time and in the course of the morning at the el-Khalayifa estate at the public cattle-market in the neighbourhood of Gheit el-Enab in the district of Karmuz in Alexandria there will be a public sale of cattle the property of Mahmud Abu Gheita of this neighbourhood in compliance with regulation 1216 in discharge of a debt of 284 piastres not inclusive of expenses incurred in the sale at the request of Mustafa Effendi Abd el-Aziz el-Sharidi merchant of Karmuz and it is incumbent on those who wish to buy to be present – Uncle Mahmud the advocate appealed against this: haven't we paid you the deposit everything will be finished in two hours, come and have dinner with us, I've killed a duck to do you proud – Abu Ibrahim! Yesterday we sent a wire to the Minister of Justice himself and on your dear life in *al-Musawwar* magazine there was a piece by Hasan Mustafa in Alexandria on 10 April 1987 saying that dying had become more expensive than living; in the graveyards of Karmuz and Sidi Bishr and Pompey's Pillar the gravediggers demand two thousand pounds for one burial. Some of them, furthermore, take the body out the very same night and sell it to the students at the Alexandria Medical School – by the piece! All heads crane towards the wall as if it were Mecca or the wailing wall or the holy altar, and in the middle of the great stones there is a high window crowded with heads I can hardly see my father's head squashed against the bars amongst all the other faces, still with all his pride, and my mother amidst all the screams and yelling calls, 'Be strong, Abu Amin! We'll be all right – don't worry about us! Look after yourself, you are all we have – O God, may you come out safe and sound!' I can still see the face of Joseph the carpenter; it used to hang in the hall of our house – in house after house after house without a break – all the years of my boyhood, my youth, my manhood: where has it gone now? I cannot find it. The glass in the thick frame of pale wood gleamed over the rough papery background which looked thick, as if it were a valuable antique canvas; the holy husband of the Virgin Mary, the husband who had not touched a hair on her head, his face all fine furrowed lines, had a special beauty; and the lineaments of his face are clear sharp and radiant as he bends over the baby Jesus: 'Lord, now lettest thou thy servant depart in peace for mine eyes have seen thy salvation.' All your life you have remained captive struggling for liberty with a hero's courage with the endurance of Upper Egyptians behind your changing and ever-present bars, and you have surely found no salvation. *Al-Akhbar* newspaper, on 17 June 1987 announced that a factory owner in el-Mahalla had been charged with defrauding an Alexandrian bank of ten million pounds by means of cheques which, it transpired, had no covering funds. *Al-Ahram* newspaper, on 13 May 1948 announced that it had drawn our attention the previous day to the arrest of Ahmad Misri, barber, on board an Egyptian ship because of the Communist and Socialist literature found in his cabin; and that today Mr Mustafa Salim the magistrate of Summary Justice had ordered the release of the aforementioned individual on bail while the investigation was being carried out.

Was it Cousin Witwat who came with me? I can see his face now, shining and dark as milky coffee. We didn't say anything to anyone. We didn't ask permission. We just went off to the Concordia Cinema in *shari'* Muhammad Sa'id – me, the puritanical boy who had waited seven years for the sacrament of baptism fearing every day that he would die before he became a true Christian and go to Purgatory and be denied the Kingdom of Heaven for ever, who wished to be so holy that not one page of his life on earth would be blotted before he saw the face of God. This boy, I, saved milliemes from my pocket money until I had the price of a ticket, thirteen milliemes in total, and then I went, with Cousin Witwat, from three o'clock to six, to see Tarzan. My heart beat for Jane, I wept with pity for her as the huge elephant came trampling through the jungle to attack the band of baddies, and how we laughed at the rascally Chita. When we got home I found that they had turned the house upside-down looking for us. When my mother asked me I told her everything but my honest confession did me no good at all. I found myself tied by a rope to a brass bedpost in the big bedroom. The rope cut into my ankles and wrists and hugged my middle suffocatingly. The pangs of injustice and trial were far worse than the hot sting of the slipper all over my body.

The No. 5 kerosene lamp cast its meagre yellow-tongued light over the bedroom. No one had come in. I had been banished, abandoned in pain and rejection. I dozed, only to be roused once more by stabs of agony, by the dearth of sympathy, the awareness of injustice, the sawing of the rope and the wobbliness in my legs and middle caused by the bedpost crucifixion. I had returned to the inextinguishable fire of the dream and the pecking eagles ate away at my liver.

My father came home very late at night, which was usual during that period. He was accountant to several shops in Kom el-Nadura and el-Labban. He released me without fuss. He told me to sit down and have something to eat, and sat beside me on the pallet as I took morsels of food from the little table in front of us – to please him, not from hunger, which he realized.

That child who did not weep or cry out, who did not for an instant ask for mercy, who ground his teeth and squeezed his eyes tight shut, who found obscure consolation in the agonies of the martyrs – only at bedtime did he give way to the tears he had held in check. In the darkness of his bed he stifled his sobs for fear his two little sisters beside him would wake. How he has wept all his life under the covers, with the same sense of injustice – for himself, his country and people, for the poor, the prisoners, the persecuted, the voiceless, the rest. What a heavy price he has paid for his dreams – and he did not ask for a thing in return.

At least, that is what he said.

The demonstration had come out of the factory at the end of *shari'* Karmuz. The students were approaching from the direction of Muharram Bey. A detachment of Security Force troops had lined up at the junction of the two large streets, not far from the red-brick Anglican Church. They had green wooden riot shields slung over their arms and old-fashioned long rifles in their hands.

I had been up all night, moving from Bab Sidra to *shari'* el-Harrasa to Sidi Kireyim, calling on our few comrades from the factory at their houses. We talked in the yards or even the street outside where they had set up little ovens and braziers, and where chickens and ducklings ran about. They had brought their country ways with them.

As for the students, we had decided at the committee meeting that they would be the responsibility of Qasim Ishaq. Early in the morning, after two or three hours' sleep I went out. My job was to observe the progress of the demonstration. If anything unforeseen happened I was to cut down through the potters' yard and inform Qasim, who was stationed at the top of Abbasiya Hill. This arrangement was difficult, taxing and inadequate but it was all we had in our power to devise, since we didn't even have a bicycle.

The streets were deserted now. Empty suddenly of the small groups of people who had been roaming the quarter since the early hours, chanting, 'My country, my country! Forward, forward, soldiers of sacrifice! Onward to victory under the flag!' Nor did they stop at that: 'Peace to our country!' they cried, and

'Long live the people!' instead of 'Long live our king!', which back then was so reckless in its disregard of the consequences as to be tantamount to revolution. It had been agreed upon among the representatives of the various committees, unions and alliances that we should distance our groups and thus the whole demonstration from such blatant and inflammatory slogan-chanting. We did not want to goad the soldiers gathered at the crossroads in Government Security Force lorries and goods trucks hired from the people.

Even so, some of the groups were shouting, 'God is great! The Quran is our constitution and the Prophet our leader!' The shops had closed their doors and pulled down the iron shutters. The tram which swayed clanging down the now-deserted *shari'* Raghib Pasha had no everyday passengers on it; it was occupied entirely by shouting demonstrators waving their triple-starred green flags. The shouting became more agitated and confused. 'Evacuation evacuation government is government by the people down with colonialism down with occupation long live the union of students and workers total evacuation or death down with Sidqui down with Bevin glory to Egypt God is great Ismail was a true prophet long live the people glory to Egypt.' The demonstration had gone beyond the bounds of planning or control.

The crowds had begun to approach from Karmuz. They were nearly at Muharram Bey now. The students' shouts could be heard in the distance, roaring but indistinct; they were more coordinated now, swelling and vigorous. It shook my heart, it had a strange swirling echo in the empty street. It had power, it had authority, and I loved it.

I heard several terse indistinct commands. Suddenly gunshots cracked through the air. Scattered seemingly-benign shots, hollow 'pops' vanishing harmlessly into the air. Then in the middle of the road I saw two, three people twitch and then quietly keel over. And then I couldn't hear anything any more. It was as if total silence had suddenly fallen. I saw rows of people surging together, thronging in tumult, spreading and reforming and then scattering once more to fall one after the other to the ground. The soldiers were down on one knee now, the officer behind them raising his pistol aloft. The long rifles were trained on the heart of the crowd. I saw people take those who had fallen to the tarmac and lift them on to their shoulders, into their arms, and carry them at a run towards the alleys branching off *shari'* No. 12 and *shari'* Raghib Pasha. The ranks of people had broken up now and the junction was deserted but all of a sudden I dashed into the middle of the road without a single conscious thought of what I was doing. I had seen Gamalat. Mona's sister Gamalat who lived in our building in *haret* el-Gullanar. She was sprawled on the ground. Her face had a doughy pallor and one arm was twisted beneath her body which had hit the road without a sound. Her skirt had ridden up and she was only wearing one shoe – her other foot was all bare.

I can still feel her in my arms now, Gamalat's body warm and limp in my arms, a thread of blood streaming slowly from the corner of her mouth, her beautiful eyes widened in amazement and still filled with the light of life which I had thought would never go out. But death was not beautiful. She was a deadweight, horribly slack. Life was leaving her; I told myself that maybe she was only injured, she was only unconscious, that she would come back, but I could not convince myself. There was a factory worker – I could tell from the way he looked and acted – who was carrying her with me; what did I say to him? Can I remember? We made for her house at a run – I didn't know if she still lived there but I was acting without thinking. When her mother opened the door I felt myself collapse to the ground. Everything went black, a pitch-black shot with the red of my closed lids. Here I was, I thought bitterly, in the gloomy hallway I had known so long as a boy, scene of my snatched kiss on Mona's cheek when my arm was around her waist. I was panting and gasping, hardly able to draw breath, my chest threatening to explode for want of air. I was angry because I could do nothing but struggle to breathe, I could not help but live still, I continued to exist.

Strange things, meaningless things. People, cars, trams, buses, lories coming down the streets branching from the old Raml station into roads bordering and overlooking the sea. I see them from the wide glass-fronted balcony of the Casablanca Café. The red dusk streaks the clouds, the clouds are flooded with the slow fire of the horizon behind the fortress of Qaitbay. My heart is racked with pain for old loves. As for death, life, justice, affection, I convince myself that they doubtless have value. As for the sun bathing the blank walls of the houses on the Corniche, the brilliant blue of the sea I know no truth in it, I see no light in it. They come from an alien star, the passions of the clinging vine; they are now withered and fallen along with the dashed hopes of the dream, the love denied to leave only the glinting embers of tears under cover of night. Why since they have gone do I proclaim them now? Raml station is bathed in the twilight's glow. Your voice is gone from me but my love will not die.

Sparks on the border of the sky's weave lit with the sky's fire, a heaven shattered but revolving still to dredge the lees of memories borne floating on the flood-tide's silent foam, a dumb imprisoned tempest. Will these tears not cease, will they not abate? The white nun seated opposite me in the tram to Bacchus looks at me somewhat astonished, perhaps tenderly. The tears mingle with my blood, I cannot help them, a strange silence now reigns in the tram, no one is looking at the man overcome by noiseless seeming-intolerable weeping. He gets out before the stop, out into the empty streets between Shallalat and the long cemetery wall. The sea-breeze comes to him from afar and there is a breath of the thwarted dream in the blowing of the wind: 'You don't love me.'

And what of all this?

A gust blows a leaf against the unyielding wall of silence. A yellow-green leaf not yet dried, still some blood there in those fine veins.

Who knows what they contain, the hidden places of the spirit?

6

Imperial Palms of Barren Beauty

'You go on in,' I said to my friend George. 'I'll wait for you by the door.'

The door was made of pale carved wood with a fan-light above. The grainy glass behind the thin bars was painted a restrained dark blue and covered with thick criss-crosses of sticky yellow paper.

In front of the wooden door the short sandy path where I stood led down to a small iron gate set in the middle of a low stone wall.

And to the right of the door a single tall palm tree sprouted from the path, shaggy spiky scales of bark curling from the tatty trunk, long dark brown tufts dangling beneath the bunches of dates. The high crown overshadowed the roof of the building.

The little alleyway was narrow but clean and quiet. We had approached it from *shari'* Ambroise Rallye in the district called Little Sporting. Inside the building the stairs were made of marble, mopped with care and bathed in the Sunday early afternoon light. House-plants were ranged across the wide tiles on either side of the ground-floor hallway. Their big leaves thrusted up from clay pots placed inside yellowly-gleaming bulging copper tubs.

George had come to our house in *shari'* Ibn Zahar in Raghib Pasha. My mother roused me from a heavy troubled afternoon sleep. George and I made for the Corniche on foot.

'Where are we going?' he asked.

'To the Plague, of course,' I replied.

'You've reminded me,' he said. 'I've got to meet someone. She's here in Little Sporting.'

'What's that got to do with me?'

'Just come along,' said George.

The Corniche was almost deserted. At intervals we passed people selling roast corn on the cob, arranging their goods and making neat stacks of little black chunks of charcoal. English, Afrikaaner and Sikh soldiers loafed about or piled into gharries which passed at a gallop as each group tried to put distance between it and the one behind.

The shushing of the sea below damped the hot afternoon and gave it a rhythm.

'She stays at home with her mother,' said George. 'Doddery old Armenian hag. Her father's Greek, he's in prison. Do you remember the mutiny on board the Greek ships?

'She's a cutie, really,' he continued. 'Still green. Still got her cherry, if you know what I mean.'

'You go on in,' I said. 'I'll wait for you by the door.' I had a fair idea of the kind of women George had dealings with, but I couldn't entirely believe it. They were a particular kind of women, very well-known. Italians, Greeks, Armenians, all doubtless just trying to get by, I told myself, with no other way to do it. Most of them, anyway; there were some who must have been out for a bit of an adventure, a sexual thrill, not to mention the valuable temptations of nylon tights, rations of cigarettes, camel-hair blankets and ladies' gifts from the army and navy warehouses.

Some of these women came with George to the roller-skating arena which was a preferred meeting-place. We called it by the nickname 'the Plague'. But most of George's dealings took place without further ado in the small – or sometimes large – houses dotted around the side-streets of Raml.

She was coming down the stairs when I saw her. Screwing

up her eyes a bit, dazzled a bit by the light pouring in through the door. Hesitant, obviously scared, also defiant. I could not see the expression on George's face as he came down behind her, but his hand on her hip told me enough.

He did not bother to introduce me by name. He said simply in French, 'My friend.'

And announced her off-handedly as 'Sylvana'.

There was a very fine down above her full freshly red-painted top lip, I noticed. Her lower lip was delicate and sharply-drawn. She had very thin, almost scrawny arms and legs. I could see that her whole outfit – the blue blouse of shiny imitation silk, short flimsy red skirt, and scarf made from the skirt-fabric and tied over her hair – had been run up at home especially for this new career. Her shoes were white, with wedge heels.

The thought came and went. 'Her father's in prison, and her mother . . .'

Et cetera. Why go on? It's a dull tale, often told. Even the ending is dull.

In my naïve boyish way I said: But that doesn't make it any the less tragic.

And I said: Good heavens, the tragedy is all in my mind. She doesn't know what is tragic about all this – and even if she did she wouldn't care.

So why this anxious, this almost pleading look? And why all this near-contemptuous, no, near-reckless boldness? This determination to survive ruin?

Her hair beneath the light red scarf was slightly bushy, fluffed out either side of her head like a fan. Her small breasts were pert and bra-less under the shiny blue blouse. Blindly she took the last but one step, George propelling her gently but firmly. I saw the hot glare of the street between her long almost emaciated legs.

George did not buy a ticket at the entrance to the roller-skating park. Everybody knew him there. We all went in for free.

There was an onslaught of noise, the bump and clatter of skates travelling over the narrow gaps between the white tiles, the pounding driving rhythm of very loud music. Speaking had become impossible, which was just as well. What could one say?

The big burly Australian soldier was waiting for us. 'Hello Johnny,' said George. How could I get myself out of this? An empty Sinalco pop bottle stood on the small round marble table in front of him, next to his wide-brimmed hat, and there was also a tumbler full of extremely pale liquid. The smell of gin was strong and unmistakable. The soldier's eyes had started to redden and wander a little.

The skating park lay between the Sporting Cinema and a walled area of waste ground. Low dark houses backed on to the park. Round bathroom windows, as well-fitted as steamer portholes, formed the only break in the walls which were traversed by waste and water-pipes, thick ones and thin ones, and drain pipes from the roofs. The floor of the skating arena was made of large square paving-stones with very thin cracks between them; it was this which caused the continual piercing noise as the metal skate wheels went over them like little railway trains, interweaving and rushing as fast as they could.

I sat down, completely unrelaxed in this intolerable musical din. The girls on their little wheels were turning in circles, gliding, standing tall, dancing, swaying. They were leaning over and righting themselves, stumbling and steadying, flying like birds, their arms outstretched for balance and covered by wide-sleeved blouses, their skirts riding up and spread out tight by calves and thighs which were slim and slender or plump and chubby – sometimes revealing for an instant, as they spun in a circle, a little intimate brightly-coloured flash. Their knees were round and smooth or knobbly and rough-looking; they were Syrian, Maltese, Greek, they were accompanied by the few foreign schoolboys, English soldiers in khakhi shorts, Afrikaaners and coal-black Senegalese in all the different colours, initials and insignia of their various uniforms. There were some brown heavy-featured girls there, with dyed hair and the lips of countrywomen, and there was no mistaking their profession any more than that of the men who were watching them like sordid vultures from the seating area, scattered with little round tables, which surrounded the arena.

She had fixed on her skates and was about to go out into the arena when she paused and turned to me.

'Did you know,' she said, 'my father's from Crete?' She was speaking French, using *tu*. My knowledge of French at the time was limited.

'Crete?' I said.

'Yes.'

She brought her face up close to mine, balancing on only two wheels. Suddenly she kissed me on the mouth. Tenderly, almost gratefully.

'Promise me one thing,' she said.

'What?'

'Leave me alone. I don't want anything to do with you. Ever. Go away. Don't concern yourself with me.'

'Yes, Sylvana,' I said.

George and his Australian friend were gaping at us.

I left quickly without saying goodbye to any of them. I walked along the Corniche for a very long time, until the great ember of the sun had been doused in the sea and it was evening.

We were standing by the iron fence bordering the Corniche at Sidi Bishr, myself and my friend Ahmad Sabri the artist who later went to Paris and studied under Loth, married an American and lived in Mallorca when it was still a wild and lonely island, and who even in his late sixties was hale and vigorous. We used to watch the girls, local Alexandrians and summer holidaymakers as they crossed in a continuous procession between the cars which back then were not all that numerous, past the sellers of roast corn on the cob, lupine, melon-seeds and fenugreek, ice-cream, peanuts and coloured balloons, earrings, glass bangles and strings of fake beads. Ahmad Sabri teased them in a suave and witty manner which for the most part brought furtive smiles and sometimes direct looks in which an element of cautious invitation could be discerned.

Ishaq Bey Hilmi, the former cross-channel hero and Inspector of Beaches, had issued summer regulations to the effect that it was forbidden to wear bathing-costumes as indecent as those worn by public entertainers. Women's attire must be long enough to cover the upper thigh even if they showed a modest expanse of midriff. Bikinis were still unimaginable; the bomb had not been dropped yet.

She must have been thirteen or so, stooped over by the water's edge looking for clams and little empty snail-shells. She looked very Upper Egyptian standing there, lifting her shirt above the water to bare her thin dark calves. She called out suddenly under the distant sky in the quiet of the sunlit early morning: 'Ireni! Ireni!'

Her friend − or her sister − came running, smaller and slighter, scampering over the wet sand.

'Didn't I tell you we'd find one, with Christ's permission?'

In her hand she was holding a large white spiral shell which gleamed in the mysterious sound of the light.

Where are the savage rocks at el-Shatbi and Cleopatra and Sidi Gaber, rough and sandy, stony ochre, all tiny holes, wild and unruly? No beach huts there, only an escarpment where fragile molluscs crawled and little near-translucent crabs scuttled towards their cracks and crannies. Beneath the gentle slope of the rocky hillocks there is a shelf where the shaggy seaweed piles layer on layer, sticky and acrid.

Sometimes we used to deceive our hearts with apparitions around the bleak rocks rising from the waves of the sea-tempests, the spirit's churning foam.

Why does it appear to me even now, that marble stairway at

Little Sporting, descending for ever and never reaching the ground?

Sylvana in the grip of her despair, courtesan at the Scarabee.

Su'ad as-Samahi, tall and elegant and fastidiously dressed, from the ancient aristocracy of Bahari, her face a smooth narrow oval, her eyes hollow and somewhat inward-looking in their deep sockets with a special mysterious attraction. She knew how I loved her friend and she seemed to encourage me and give me her blessing with her look and her wordless smile. She married an appeal judge and went to live in Iraq long before the rush to leave began.

Despina in the Accounts Department, dainty as a doll or toy, always perfectly made-up. She hardly knew any Arabic at all, she sped impatiently about as if the world were in danger of slipping away from her, and her beefy Greek fiancé would be waiting for her by the door at five on the dot each afternoon, and she hung on his arm as if her feet were not touching the ground.

Zizi, nameless so long in my mind, no stock of love for her laid up; only the special honour which could not be violated, not even in the bars of Bab el-Karrasta or the promenade cafés of Stanley.

Sitt Wahiba to whom I was the darling son she jealously guarded against the girl who journeyed by night – guarded to the point of betraying the girl and surrendering her near enough to perdition.

Iskandara with whom I sank beneath the sea-vine, her long hair aglow in the candlelight, in the glitter of the salt-swell.

Yvette Sassoon abounding with life, round face, round curves, hair the colour of raw chestnuts, full of last night's fun – the telephone at work never stops ringing for her, and seated beside me she replies to them all in the whole range of Alexandrian idioms, all kinds of sweet talk, whispered or frank, coy or licentious, cheery or mournful.

Playful Mona, heart-hidden, looking at me with her slightly

pop-eyes, her turtle eyes articulating a desire I cannot assuage, and Gamalat the martyr whose body I carried in my arms as the chill of death crept in.

Aunt Wadida, fiery-eyed and sharp-tongued, kind to me; my boyhood's dawn bewitched by her lingerie, her lacy gauzy brassières dripping on the line.

Aunt Ester my eyes closed against her thighs staunching my tears so that I fell into a deep sleep after the girl threw herself from the school window to fall on the paving-stones opposite our old house.

Sumaya the despairing poet's girl, the Englishwoman's daughter – my friend Ramzi killed himself for love of her; for love of her and despair of the world.

Janine the Yugoslavian for whom my friend Philippe Nakhla embezzled, who deserted him after he was found out, and he died of tuberculosis a short while later.

The lady Nagiya, she with the serpent cached betwen her breasts, Coptic eyes in a face taken from a sarcophagus in the Fayyum.

Umm Toto, wand-slim Diana, my childhood's dawn fell tangled in her sensual net; the knowledge shocked him; he never escaped her snare.

Layla fantasmal Bedouin, she with the ring piercing her nose and the dark red ribbon over her shining dark forehead; her bosom proudly carried she comes accompanied by the smell of sheep and goats and the unending beat of poetry.

Nefisa charged with explosive power writhing in the dust in physical agony, the imaginary toils of labour which alone were true.

Rana murdered at Sidi Bishr – who killed her? Her straight-backed Upper Egyptian lover? Floating for ever on the surging high seas of passion.

Susu, pupil at the Nabawiya Musa School whom I sheltered from the rainstorm – I dashed my own hopes by telling her my name which I have so long denied and whose echo resounds in my streets.

Madeleine and Miryam the inseparable sisters who walked about in Raml station – we used to watch them from the windows of cafés, the Ala Keifak or the Casablanca. All eyes were on them when they passed by, their black hair flowing loose down their backs, for when they walked they hardly moved their arms, and it was that stiff wooden gait still somehow fluid which was enchanting, which left no one uncaptivated. Madeleine married and went to live in America. I saw her thirty years later in Florida, a woman in her prime whose eyes were still the same, a merry grandmother. As for Miryam, she fell in love with a Canadian Jew and lived with him in Toronto. She never got married. She never had any children. I never saw her again.

Umm Dawlat who lived in the flat below, who used to send me notes hidden in the pages of paperbacks *Darling my dearest darling I don't go to sleep at night until you come back, only then do I go to bed with dreams of my love.*

The silent Madonna of Ghobrial who appears still in my dreams bathed in inextinguishable light.

Aunt Sara just a few years older than me; I clung to her at night on top of the oven in the hall in the cold autumn out at Tarrana, when all the girls of the Thousand and One Nights from Baghdad to Samarkand prowled around me.

Katrina the ninth tree dual and eightfold precious, whose hymn is endless.

Yvonne Naqqash in the Fax school learning French in the afternoon and in my dream baring her breasts to the wafting sea-breeze: two fruits brimming with rich pent sap.

And the girl in the blue silk robe on the balcony of the house in Muharram Bey, a riddle still unlocked.

Stepho the Greek girl with the splendid overwhelming bosom and yet she had a lovely carriage, a light step, lips permanently parted in a smile. My friend Salim Andrawos called her 'the cow' in three languages, and when this nickname spread throughout the company she seemed almost to approve, for she never got cross or scowled at us. Her occasional smiling glances in our direction came as unstinted as before.

We greeted her – it was our first wedding anniversary – on our way to Manolides' Bakery in Ibrahimiya to buy bread for Easter Day, special bread made with eggs with a silver coin in the middle bringing luck to the finder. Easter greetings in French, Greek, Arabic, the joyful festival air of Easter Saturday morning – all this is also a blessing gone never to return. Afterwards we went to Monachos' on the next block and bought a dozen assorted cakes for twenty-five piastres because I said 'keep the change' to the brown-faced assistant in the spotless white coat. My friend the little ragamuffin newspaper vendor yelled '*Ahram Gumhuriya Tachodromos Progres Ahram*', as he skipped over the tramlines while in the distance the tram appeared with a majestic stately clanging of its bell, a clean blue tram with people leaning gaily down from the top deck.

Demure soft-spoken Odette. I had a date with her. Hot and bothered I bellowed for my sister. 'Aida! I'm in a hurry! Where's my shirt!'

Out she dashed in her slippers and housedress, returning a few moments later with the shirt washed and ironed and the collar starched. This estimable engineer, now employed by the Graeco-Roman Museum, had exactly three shirts and two suits, one light, one dark. No sooner did I get home than my mother or sister, every single day of the week, early or late, took my shirt and washed it, to take it the following day when it was dry to the laundryman so that it came back with a white starched collar.

I walked from *shari'* Raghib Pasha to the Fuad Cinema for the three o'clock showing, careful that my shoes stayed shiny. I found her already waiting for me in the foyer, her bobbed hair, her tentative smile.

'Do you like my new suit?' she asked. 'I'm wearing it specially for you.'

In the darkness of the cinema she held my hand. I put my hand in her lap to feel the softness of her thigh. Afterwards we went to the Scarabee on Stanley Bay to have a Cinzano or a Martini, very dry, above the wintry blue of the sea. This excursion emptied my pockets. The following day I would borrow the usual pound from my friend Antoine who used to work with me years ago at the British Navy depot in Kafr Ashri. Antoine, who was Odette's brother, did not know or pretended not to know – I'm not sure which – that I was taking her out. I didn't find that the least embarrassing, although I had a slight feeling of transgression.

As for her sister Arlette, a very tall girl with long unstyled hair who always looked at me wth a wondering wordless expectation – I kissed her once, on the cheek, after we had been having a drink on Christmas Night, and her hair fell over my face. I never kissed Odette's lips. I had yearned so long for her mouth but never so much as tasted it. Arlette went to Brazil. She married a relation of hers, a Syrian Brazilian businessman. A few years later I lost touch with them all.

After 1956 they all left, nearly all of them, for Athens, Rome or Marseilles: Yvette Sassoon and Marcel Sadduq, Stepho Orphanides, Despina Stamatopolo, Rita and her husband Pissas, Anastasia and her husband Dimitri Campanis, tough old Maria Simonides, Janine Birkowitz, Madeleine and Miryam and Antoine and Odette and Arlette. But George Skiryanides refused to leave. I saw him in the late seventies. He was coming out of the billiard hall in *shari'* Safiya Zaghlul. It was summer and he was in short sleeves, he had a brisk old man's walk.

My enduring Ni'ma my homeland, my refuge in my permanent exile my one diamond in Athenios–*shari'* Fuad. Mornings standing like tombstones, numberless, my music swells and disperses against the walls of the spirit. The newspaper-vendor in front of Pâtisserie Bodrot is forever holding out to me a news-

102

paper with no date on it a shudder of the fire of morning dew, the violence of the fever of despair, desire and grieving a gloomy fire a millefeuille pastry and my passionate fingers trace their appeal over your cheeks a thousand times and pause on the border of your lips the last tram to Cleopatra Hammamat Bach's toccata and fugue no. 545 in F major plants curling on either side of your neck delirium of drunkenness at the music of your body and my lips brush the little scar beneath your right ear. You are with me. I have no choice. You girl of Alexandria, single however many you are; too many for me. You force me to silence. And in the end is there anything else but silence, however long my Alexandrian songs are sung, silence to the end of time?

O girls of Alexandria, your lips are sugar-sweet.

Has the world filled up with yesterday? Yesterday brims over!

The Nijrani palm the sight of her glimpsed on the crowded shore of Ma'moura beach an unmitigated agony and pain. She did not see me and she did not know I could see her. Beneath the clusters of wide beach umbrellas she sat surrounded by her men as always – dark men, muscular men on their faces the stamp of power and money. And she was ruler – as always – over them all, with this explosive femaleness which exuded from every pore of her body even when she was fully clothed on the beach. And her conversation! Eternal enchanting Shahra-zad, the men were enthralled, captive to Circe their souls the spirits of pigs, the lioness Sekhmet Bist from the jungles of Fatimid Cairo and the ruins of Sharqiya and Nag Hammadi. She said she had studied at Victoria College for Girls in Alexandria but she had always remained a stranger to Alexandria. Mistress of sexual pain of the transports of sensual delight – and what of her kindness? Why are you so hard on her, this paradis-aical lady whose choicest nectar you have sipped? Who has bestowed on you her love and the tenderness of her bosom,

103

that granted to none human, that which will shield you forever from the injury of all worlds?

Imperial palm soaring smooth-limbed, clear-skinned brown, long leaf-tresses pinnate green, something vicious in the spikes of those soft buds, how sweet to be lulled by massage so good to the touch, compliantly swinging in my arms feeling secure and provoking a gush from the well-spring of passion very close to my eyes, very close to my breast to the column of carnal desire. Short palm trees line the Mahmudiya Canal as it if leads to an individual private Serapeum or to a personal Alexandrian Karnak whose palatial pillars stand unrelentingly firm, tumble constantly down. Her round breasts laden with date-clusters lush black and syrupy sweet my lips suck and suckle unsated at the sugar. Round bony clusters, the tresses of seduction burst unfaltering from them, sunshot beams, the stab of solid soft vegetable spikes.

Their beauty endures
Barren

When I went to the fortress of Qaitbay at Anfushi it was wrecked and the stones were scattered everywhere. I saw that the imperial palms had dried up. Their pillars were scorched and black, their tufts lank and drooping, their broad leaves withered. Where are the glad fertile groves of Egyptian palms, the joyful clusters of red dates? When did they sink beneath the sands of Sidi Bishr, the tumbling dunes? Massed in the moonlight they threw shadows over the fragile-pliable body of the sand, shadows which veiled me in a special whispered hardly-audible soughing, in the silver of the magic idol orbiting above. And at high noon they had been my refuge from the August heat when breaths of faint fresh palm-leaf perfume

104

gusted beneath the sun-dappled veil of shadow; utter ecstasy of the senses, ecstasy of the heart.

I have no choice.

The piles of fishnets were soft-woven heaps, a faded white the colour of old dough. The folds hung down, redolent of fish, over the dry upturned hulls of the boats on the coarse sand of the shore. There was a big dog there, a bitch with hanging dugs, following a brown-chested brawny young fisherman into the sea. He was swimming out into the leaden-green swell, and occasionally he turned and scolded the dog, waving her back with one hand; I could not hear his voice. The dog ploughed on after him, placid and trusting, without making a single splash or spot of foam on the calm languid waves.

I read in *al-Basir* that a teacher had been found murdered in her house in the Ghobrial area. A legless beggar had been charged. I felt as if leaves of eternal life had been stripped from the body of purity, that a defilement had been accomplished which could never be washed away or purified. The fire was in my mind, the fire of the potters' hill in the twilight of Ghobrial which was like an anteroom of Hell thronged with the shades of our betrayals, our blasphemies, our broken promises. And the darkened buildings confirm me in this for they are dumb and shut up in the winter of the Corniche, peeling as if leprosy has taken hold, the ironwork the rusty red-brown of decaying bones, grinning skeletons whose flesh has been torn away and scattered to the winds.

She told me that in 1942 the house in *shari'* Bubastis was new. There was a little green garden lying between their house and the tall building next door where an Italian family lived. The father, Signor Lafonti was in prison. He had worn a black shirt before the war and led a group of Fascists in Alexandria.

His wife Sitt Teresa scraped along by selling bottles of watered-down brandy to the grocers and the English soldiers who came and went. She stuck the labels of well-known makes on the bottles. She had two girls and a boy the same age as the soldiers. She said the soldiers used to taunt them when they were sitting out on their ground-floor patio by singing:

'*Uno giorno Mussolini vol fare l'aviatore*
'*Monchata di benzini pissata so'l motore*'

whereupon the girls and the boy came down from their terrace and immediately threw themselves into a brawl of fists, kicking, hair-pulling, rolling on the green grass of the little garden until the adults came to break up the fight. Then afterwards they had a game of *siga* together as if nothing had happened – that or an afternoon dip under the rock at Sidi Gaber.

The bullets came out fast, glinting in the morning light, from the English military police sentry-box. It was locked from the outside and stood beneath the huge statue of Sa'd Zaghlul who seemed to be distant and aloof from what was happening. The open jeep was parked on the Corniche. There were four soldiers inside, calm and steady-looking. Each one had a tommy-gun pointed in our direction as we walked in procession around the sentry-box and circled the line of garrison troops standing nearby. The boy stripped off his white gown and doused it with petrol. He threw the quickly igniting ball of fire through the window of the sentry-box, standing there afterwards in his vest and pants. Suddenly the shooting stopped. Black and white smoke poured out of the window. A roar came from the surging crowd, and shouts broke out. The jeep moved, the machine-guns chattered, some people fell, and the demonstrators broke up to regroup in *shari'* Sa'id. To whom would it have occurred that those in the sentry-box were not quite the same as rats caught in a trap? Or that murder is murder? Who could have said that to himself even if it were true?

I said: the necessity of symbols is an absolute necessity. The rule of symbols cannot be toppled. Symbols do not tolerate questioning.

I said: Values disintegrate in historic hours. History has other values.

I said: True, even if tyrants justify themselves this way.

And at the pouring-out of the night a lone star signalled to me. Were we at the beginning? No beginning and no end. The sky is thick and velvety lining the full breasts with the dyed yellow parachute-silk wrapped around the body between bursts of ack-ack fire and beneath the eyes of Greek soldiers on watch in the British Navy depot between the searchlights raking the dome of the sky and strips of motionless froth thrown now over the buttock cheeks cloven sweetly rounded over both sides of the safeguarded gorge embracing the narrow waist and muffling the whisper of the wavelets in her white embrace, and I took the crowded ferry across the Mahmudiya Canal where the brown waters rushed by a dark honey hue and I paid my two milliemes and when the hull bumped the earthen bank the impact pushed the boat out again a little way just as I was stepping off, and then the chasm of water opened up beneath my feet and then I was gasping in the heavy water and then it was the dream of drowning the body slipping in my arms water dripping from the forest of light wet hair between the young limber legs pressed together.

In the world the purity of eternity seems innocent of time. Little dark Alexandria prettied up like a girl still a maiden, a girl with the rawness of unruptured virginity about her, like a cactus with tender spines, and the tall white tapering trees which give a chilly sigh in the round piazza at Glymonopolo and we on our weaving nightly way from drinking to the glass-

107

fronted room at Stanley Bay: and she is between us, Philippe tall thin bony-faced and tubby Thomas with his little paunch, smug Thomas, and me with my head awhirl rising and falling angry and earnest and dreaming and curled upon an as yet unripened decision.

I slid with nocturnal glee down the lamp-post, where the gaslight quivered behind the thick faceted glass, outside my aunt Hanuna's house in *shari'* Sidi Kireyim. The flame flickered as the lithe form of Witwat came down the post after me, his long tunic rucked up above his shiny *café-au-lait* legs, legs the tram-wheels crushed that summer, soon afterwards; and my lone star twinkles at me and guards me from an unpleasant fate and in the celestial pin-pricks of starlight the boys take off all their clothes and leave them rolled in balls on the precisely chiselled concrete cubes which are darker and more knobbled in their stark nocturnal nudity. We haggle with the cold girl, the clearly hungry girl, we drive a hard bargain with our few piastres, and there is something of a desire for humiliation and revenge which is not hidden from our minds, blurred though they are with thirstily drunk beer from Lorantos's in Safiya Zaghlul next to the Rialto Cinema.

At the civil court today, presided over by Mr Muhammad Hafiz, an individual by the name of Fathy el-Sayyid Abbas was charged that on 5 March 1942 he did purposefully damage a British Army vehicle by pouring petrol over it and setting fire to it. The judge decided to adjourn the case until 1 June and to transfer it to the court of Summary Justice which dealt especially with offences connected with demonstrations, after the President of the Jordanian Lawyers' Syndicate had stated that the charge levelled at the defendants was nothing more than the duty of every Arab citizen, for the sons of the Arab people had learned that they must banish, struggle against the Israeli occupation in every shape or form: and as for the charges against the heroes of Sawrat Masr or the Egyptian Revolutionary Movement he hoped to share in the same. Car-bodies burn with black fire and children muffled in distinctive *kuffiyehs* throw stones, and soldiers muffled in metal helmets throw gas cylinders whose choking white fumes rise in the narrow alleys between long stone walls and the newscaster says impartially almost without concern: ' . . . which brings the number martyred in the Intifada to 329'.

As for the hubbub of the world, the people, the pillars of the Corniche painted pale blue, people shut in their cars in the cold, I say to myself they have no meaning and I say I am alone always alone.

Yellow strips of silk run between her legs to tighten over the small hot mound and trace the line between the tender twin firmness cloven and cleaving and then to dangle in noiseless play over her thighs.

When my mother said Wipe the glass of the No. 5 kerosene lamp I felt the lightness of the hollow belly of the glass, the soft rag introduced by my fingers through the narrow round nether aperture; my cloth-covered hand wiped the glass which became warm from my wiping and my gentle attentive grasp in a slow and orderly revolution, and I was immersed in silent tenderness.

White cloud-formations in the night sky behind them the hidden soaring lamp casting a diffused light and the tarmac wet with sea-moisture reflects their image and locks it within my breast.

In the fever of the frenzy of my first boyhood, in the affirmation of my boyish identity I would rain blows and slaps with the flat of my hand all over the body of my sister Aida whom I loved, and my love for her even now is troubled, and this ritual of rage was because she did not listen to what I said, because I was the oldest and what I said went for all of them; and this uproarious bout of hitting and slapping gave me a kind of fulfilment not only lustful but cosmic as well. Yet the violent striking of tender sisterly female flesh brought no physical pleasure but rather total and utter isolation. I said: Did you not say that the time for all this is past, that all of it is in vain? I said: But that does not diminish the fact that in its own way it was ugly, small, base by any standard. It is absolutely unforgivable, absolutely unjustifiable.

Wisps of marigold material over the slope of bony shoulders. Why do you come with me down every road, a pulse a squall a pang in the throat, a delirium I cannot emerge from, and is it you, you the last clarity of the sky?

High heels tap-tap and echo across the fixity of the shattered stars the detritus the ravelled radiation the tips of fine braids tickle the smooth roused supersensitive skin.

We were walking hand in hand in the early morning, a small anxious but defiant group, through the large square with its pretty green gardens. We had come from Menaché Bridge and were heading for *shari'* Fuad passing the Royal Stadium; we were singing in the empty space *Egypt be free I will be your sacrifice faith of all faiths you are dear to my heart*. I was surprised by a whiff of jasmine from behind the iron fences of the smart shuttered villas *Peace to you O Egypt* the streets deserted and the doors closed *Peace to my country* and even the fizzy-drink sellers were looking at us silently, somewhat amazed.

Your unblinking eyes deep twin pools dark green, a closed

110

secret I cannot unlock I do not know what to call it I can hardly
find it out I can hardly touch it with impassioned fingertips and
it flits from my hand away into the body of darkness and the
wild-looking water-moss in this dimness seduces with its deceptive and treacherous softness hugging the ancient wet concrete
and as for the childlike girl she accepts her degradation with a
smile of consent and submission: she knows that the lengthy
bargaining is a fiction and that there will be neither profit nor
loss and that the wounds dealt to both will be the usual ones,
banal and oft-repeated and the dove of the Holy Spirit flees
away down to the river's foam, the sweet-water shoal where
the salt waves are parted and I am still being born and dying
born and dying.

The boys walk by the water's edge where the breakers crash
with a dull roar with spume held in check. They pick their
way through the smashed crates the scraps of metal the soaked
rags beneath the concrete blocks whose solid flesh is sprayed by
pebbles and the coarse sand. They fling themselves out stark
naked into the dark waves' choler and are silent.

The yellow leather straps bind the chubby legs bared to the
Corniche breeze, the light skirt flaps against them.

The monster feeds on my bowels your bitter name a white
crust on my dry lips and the world is a monster it is pain.

The people the sky the girl the friends the water the imperial
palms the darkened sand – ruins all.

You do not reply. Do you know?

Will there ever be a reply?

My question still stands unmoving.

Is my question the only thing to break the silence?

7

The Serpent and the Perfidious Bosom

The smell of sea and fresh raw fish hung in the muddy alleys.
Rainwater, borne on yesterday's onshore gale and ruffled still
by persistent squalls, lapped the basalt pavements.

I hurried past the low dripping houses, doing my best not
to stare into the shadowy entrance halls. They were full of
women, some busy cooking on hissing kerosene stoves which
lit up the gloomy space with a steady yellow glow, others cross-
legged in front of tin tubs scrubbing and rinsing the men's and
children's clothes. Others still were seated out on the steps,
bowed over big flat brass trays of uncooked rice and sorting the
grains carefully in the daylight. They had left their babies at
the breast as if they had forgotten all about them, about the
whole world – but I felt their eyes on me nevertheless, wide
eyes noticing and wondering.

I was on my way to the old quarter of Bahari where Qasim
Ishaq had rented a little flat, two rooms built on the roof. The
police would not find him there.

I went in through the great antique double doors. They were
very high with huge nails driven into the thick wood, one side
entrenched in the historic dust of the alley and the other
propped immovably against the ancient blackened stones of the
wall. There was a sudden damp smell and the earth in the large
shadowed courtyard was wet underfoot. I glanced up at the
stained-glass window above this inner court and saw the faintest

trace of the original bright colours. The thick accretions of dried dust along the edges of the pane had spread and run in the wake of yesterday's rain.

I skirted a high-wheeled cart with long shafts propped against the wall of the stairwell before starting up the broad spiral of the wooden staircase. Each step creaked under my tread, the planks either splintered or worn away; some had caved in completely. The thick round oak bannisters had been smoothed by years of rubbing, grasping, fingering hands, several so skewed and wobbly that they looked ready to fall out.

Qasim Ishaq opened the door after I had knocked in the way we had agreed. Three swift taps, then a pause, then another, and then a final tap shortly after that.

'Hey! What's up?' he asked, with his usual lively impatience. 'Has something happened?'

'He said 'j' for 'g' as people do down in Aswan, in the Nubian way. It was a full rich sound. Even as he formed the eager worried question, head bent forward in anxious anticipation, he had a faint involuntary smile. On his right temple, lighter than his dark face, were the two vertical tribal scars traditional in the south. He smelled of the thick brilliantine he used on his hair, which was as rough and coarse as wild esparto. I laughed at him – and got rather cross with him as well, in my young zealot's fashion, when I discovered that he spent literally hours conditioning this thicket of hair, massaging brilliantine into it before tying a cloth over his head and leaving it on like some womanish creature all the time that he was indoors.

His short white Nubian gown was blown against his body by the cold wind as I came in. He gathered it around him.

'So far so good,' I replied. 'The public prosecutor released Ahmad el-Nems and Yosri Halim without bail. Abd el-Qadir Nasrallah was detained for four more days but the lawyer says there's no case at all. Don't worry about Abd el-Qadir! *Your*

113

name didn't come up once during the investigation. So there you are, old man.'

He sat down on the cane chair, the only one in the large, bare unexpectedly warm room, behind the rickety desk piled with lawbooks, lecture notes and the drafts of a translation of *Literature and the Revolution* which he had been attempting for some months. He did not want me to collaborate on it.

He was a revolutionary. He stood firm to the end. Years later in prison he joined the Democratic Movement for National Liberation and went through the entire period of internment in the Oases Camp with dignity. When he came out of prison he worked as a lawyer in Aswan before dying of a brain tumour. I still miss him dreadfully and cannot believe he is dead. Sometimes when I go to Aswan I think I will see him.

On my way down the stairs I all but tripped and fell. My foot had slipped on one of the worn steps. The bannisters wobbled violently beneath my clinging hand, rocking me to and fro.

The door opened all of a sudden while the world was still spinning and reeling and tumbling down around me, while it seemed as if a tenebrous chasm of yawning gulfs had opened up beneath my feet. I heard her voice before I saw her – a low voice, charged with a special sensuality.

'In the name of the Cross and by the sign of the Cross! God protect you and your sister! Didn't you look where you were going, dear?'

My mother's words when I fell over as a child. When I wondered, and never asked: 'Who is this sister of mine and what has she got to do with it? I'm the one who has fallen over!'

But this voice held the sort of tenderness, the female softness I had missed from my mother who had always spoken in tones ringing with the absolute authority of mother over son, although she did share the note of worried sympathy I heard in this voice.

114

The dark face with the pointed chin looking down on me through the bannisters was a Coptic face. It could have come straight from a coffin-lid in the Fayyum – except that it was alive and fresh and the skin was as smooth and as pale as burnished gold. Her large deep-set eyes were rimmed with Egyptian kohl.

'Come in, come in, dear. My love, you're as white as a sheet. Come and have a drink of water at least . . . come, I'll make you some tea.'

Only then did I see that she had a tiny baby cradled in one arm. In the shadow I could see that the neck of her gown was open and the material was damp and slightly darker there. The strong fecund sweetish smell of mother's milk was unmistakable.

The baby's rather creased little face was squashed against her bosom. His eyes were closed and as puffy as an old man's. The fingers of his tiny hand were visible, spread out over the round-ness of her breast, peaceable and utterly secure. He was curled up in her embrace, his clammy skin looking cold. Suddenly I glimpsed, through the slit in the front of her white gown, the blue of an evil-eye talisman, a hand with little beads and fingers outspread, and a brown polished wooden crucifix.

Did I say anything?

I cannot remember.

I was sitting on the customary divan in a large, warm, peace-ful room. The rain was beating down outside and trickling in fluid lines across the large tight-shut window-panes. I had a glass of tea in my hand. The glass was hot and it steamed gently but it wasn't scalding. It flowed satisfyingly over my tongue to refresh my parched insides.

She was sitting in front of me on a cushion she had put down on a rug from Assyut. She had the baby in her arms.

I could picture her body inside the open-necked winceyette gown. A sturdy Coptic body, supple and fluid, contented, fulfil-led, relaxed. Like ancient glowing dark green diorite.

I must have told her, mustn't I? My name, my real name.

115

Do I have a real name? Do I have a name at all?

Did I forget the 'safety rules', the precautions we took against discovery?

For she was chatting away as secure and trusting as a sister, perhaps, or a special companion. As if there were a natural assumption, arising from the discovery of our shared names, that we had something in common. Or perhaps it was that immediate physical communion, that attraction between man and woman which is primal and spontaneous no matter how different their inclinations or manners, how conflicting their class background or cultural roots. In one instant we seemed to have known each other for measureless unchronicled aeons. With her I knew a warm physical companionship unquestioningly and unequivocably given, an intimate excitement devoid of the slightest tension, the most trifling demand. It was a feeling I never experienced again – except for the timeless comforts of the house on the street named after Sirius the Dog Star, still to come in time.

The baby suckled, innocence itself, at her little virginal breast.

She said that after the last raid on the Piazza, when the bomb had left a huge round hole in Kom Bikir which filled up with heavy stagnant bloody-tinted water, she had gone, fled really, to her husband's family in Damanhur. He was a carpenter, she told me, on the coal quay at the harbour. She said that Mikha'il – indicating the nursing baby with concern veiled by indifference and a slight apparent vexation – had been very poorly. But dear Shenouda her husband God spare him had insisted that she took the baby well out of danger. She said that just before they got to Abu Hummus the baby had started wheezing; his breathing was soon so laboured that his lips poor darling turned blue. She was sure he'd be taken from her on the journey, she said, before they even got to Damanhur, and the packed stifling train just kept chugging on and she with no idea what to do for her dying son and her heart breaking in pieces while her neighbours in the carriage were sucking their teeth with dismay and telling her to wet his lips with a drop of water and whispering that to quench the thirst of the dying was a merit in religion and carried a great reward.

She said the boy had not been christened yet. 'He'll die unbaptized,' she had thought. 'My poor lamb will never reach the kingdom or see the face of Our Lord, he will stay for all time in the murky shadows of the domains between Heaven and Hell.' For Father Philippus at el-Morqosia Church had told her all about it.

She said that all of a sudden Jesus inspired her. She hadn't made up her mind herself. Our Saviour had done it for her.

Of course there was no holy water on the train, she said, nothing pure – except maybe one thing.

She called on the people around her. She begged them for any sharp cutting thing, a razor, a knife, any kind of blade. A sheikh came over to her – he had a little snowy turban over his soft felt skull-cap and he had been reading the Quran all the time, she said, in a low voice as if he were praying to God to deliver the babe in arms. Taking a little leather case out of the pocket of his long robe, he produced a sharp razor. Take it my dear in the name of God, he told her, take it with God's blessing. She said that she took off the boy's gown, vest, pants and socks in the middle of the crush of people in the train and cradled him completely bare in her arms. Without any further ado she cut her breast. As the blood trickled out she sprinkled a few drops on Mikha'il's face and made the sign of the Cross over him, whispering, 'I baptize you in the name of the Father, the Son and the Holy Ghost. In the name of Our Lord I have made for you a perfect baptism, Mihka'il son of my womb son of Shenouda the carpenter. Lord let my body be pure of blood and milk let everything in it be pure pure pure O Lord let him deserve Thy grace and let him renounce Satan and purify his soul and body from all evil and all sin. Born again O Mikha'il son of Nagiya, son of Shenouda, son of the Lord, His be the

117

kingdom, the power and the glory for ever and ever.' Then she anointed his head with a drop of blood, a drop of milk.

She said that by the time she had dressed him and taken him once more in her arms the baby was no longer restive. No sooner did she cover her breast from the onlookers' gaze than it was healed. No sooner did the baby fall sound asleep than he was healed.

Then, she said, the whole thing was over and done with. The crowded outbound journey, the time spent far from home, the return months later to Alexandria had all occupied her mind. Her joy at her son's return to health had made her forget all about what happened in the train. So is the wisdom of the Lord when He shows us His majesty.

She said that on Christening Sunday she took him along with his father and other relatives to the great el-Morqosia Church in order to give Mikha'il a proper christening. Amidst the cries of babies, the cantors' chanting, the clash of cymbals and the handbells' chime, amidst the hymns in Coptic and Arabic, the rejoicing of the people and the blessings given by the priest as he plunged the christened children one by one into the holy water, her turn came. She held out the baby to Father Philippus. He was about to take him and dip him into the big marble basin when he stopped, his hand motionless. 'Lord Jesus!' he cried. 'The kingdom, the power and the glory be Thine for ever and ever!'

There wasn't a drop of water in the font.

The deep basin which a moment ago had been brimming with water and in which upwards of twenty babies had just that minute been baptized, was empty and gleaming and dry as a bone.

Father Philippus looked at her and at the child. His eyes were fatherly and severe, compassionate and stern.

'What is this, girl!' he said. 'Can the boy have the Devil in him? But he is innocent and without sin . . . you have not sinned, have you, my dear? Our Lord is great and the Saviour's love knows no bounds!'

Only then, she said, did she understand what had happened. She told the priest the whole story.

The boy had in truth been baptized. He had become worthy of the Kingdom of Heaven, by the blood and the milk of her breast.

Father Philippus anointed the boy's head with chrismal oil and said: 'I bless this child in the name of the Lord. Go, my girl, and pray. Our Saviour's blessing on you and your child. The boy has renounced Satan and the power of the Lord Jesus is with him.'

I could see the candles flickering around the marble font and hear the hallelujahs and hosannas shouted in praise, in joyful faith, in rejoicing at the miracle. The holy water had returned all on its own, bit by bit. No one poured it in; it had not come from any visible source. It simply welled in the smooth marble basin.

I seemed to be thinking: I believe, and at the same time: I cannot credit it.

Only then did I see that her son's mouth had been at her plump dark breast all the time. He was sucking away quite audibly, with a placid contented greed. She held him naturally to her breast, nothing lewd about the way she did it, yet it was utterly sensual. There was a long thin vertical scar on the gentle curve of her breast, whiter than the smooth golden-brown swell of the surrounding skin. A tiny gold cross she wore, lodged in the secret gorge of her cleavage, excited me.

'Lovely rich butter-biscuits!' The call came from outside the warm stuffy room where shadows flickered in the half-light of that bygone ever-present daybreak. The shutters were open a chink and the rain pattered against the wood in a wet mono-tone. My mother was still asleep. My father was not there –

119

where was he? Was he in prison over that lawsuit I never learned about until after his death? Was it my sister Aida who was enfolded in my mother's bosom, still a babe in arms, tiny, brown and crumplefaced and I loved her from when she was a few months old? Was I that young? How old – three? Is that possible? Or are the fancies of my childhood memory playing me tricks? The rich sweet taste of butter-biscuits, melting in my mouth to fill it with a milky softness, a firm doughiness in which I could feel the sugared toasted baked rose-water-scented grains of flour . . .

I positioned the chair so that I could stand on tiptoe on the seat and reach my hand up to the tin of Nadler toffees and caramels which my mother hid away on top of the high cupboard, next to the pillows and bedclothes kept for our visitors from Upper Egypt. The blue paper was stuck colourfully all around the tin and there was a picture of a heaped tumbling pile of round, oblong, hexagonal sweeties, red ones, yellow ones, brown ones and milky ones which were semi-transparent. As soon as my fingers touched the tin I drew it carefully towards me and, still perched on the chair, removed the lid. I filched two and resisted a third. I did not want my crime to be discovered – my crime which not withstanding my pious Christian ways I had forgotten was a crime. The chair wobbled and quaked beneath me, and I was aware of the ground whizzing up towards me before I landed on my head. The blow roared in my ears as if the whole world were falling down, but up I jumped straight away and, ignoring my dizziness and pain, put everything back in its place. I did not forget my haul of sweets. Were they always so dear, those sweets? So sweet because forbidden and unattainable?

'I am Muhammad Mahmud? You dog – *you* are Muhammad Mahmud! Woof woof!'

In spite of the laughter and rejoicing which the boy also thought necessary, being compared to Prime Minister Iron Fist himself, ally of the Palace and the British, was too much. He was growing up in a house where allegiance was divided between Mustafa Nahhas the leader of the Wafd party on one side of the family, and the Young Egypt party or Prince Abbas Halim on the other.

My father was a Wafd party man and always had been. As for my uncles on my mother's side, Yunan and Nathan and Surial, they were modernists and partisans of the new.

As for the boy, he earnestly and steadfastly refused to be compared with the dictator Muhammad Mahmud.

The venerable snake, the sheikh of all serpents, glided slowly over the dust in the big yard. In the middle of the yard there was a flight of wide old wooden steps.

Trusting, calm, unworried, he gazed at me. His eyes followed me as he twisted and turned across the ground which at that time was parched and cracked; one long placid flow of fat round curling body endlessly slipping over the ground, making unhurriedly for the hole, obviously his home, at the bottom of the ancient stone wall. I took refuge inside the high carriage. It had a deep round belly suspended between two magnificent, hugely high round wheels. The horse, whose great long muzzle was thrust into a nosebag, whinnied violently and gave angry snorts.

The snake had crept quietly and peacefully past, choosing his route through the dust with deliberation. He was the owner of the house while we were only strangers. He tolerated us as a casual and transient presence.

And the mouth which suckled on the milk of grief and rage from the perfidious bosom was thirsty — then and now — for the milk, the wine, the blood which is pure and unadulterated.

The queen cobra spreads her wings in tenderness. The juice of her breasts a choice wine, a lethal draught, price of godhead and poison everlasting.

A glassy look in her eyes which are kohl-rimmed for ever and fixed, the pupils drilled points.

It was the eve of Easter. We, my sister Aida and myself, were on our way to the bakery in *shari'* No. 12. Our errand was to hurry up the trays of date-cakes, cookies and rich butter-biscuits my mother had sent to be baked there. We were to say to the baker: my mother sends her greetings and says that we aren't to go home without the baker-boy carrying our full trays on his head all hot and smelling of baking fresh from the oven. And the baker would bellow at us half in earnest, half-knowing that we'd not leave without the spoils and promises of the feast. He was happy as well, partly for us but also because his pockets were jingling with festival silver.

We played for a while until the baking was done. The big warm bakery was full of sacks of flour piled in the darkness of the interior far from the blazing aperture where the crackle of the flames rose and fell, and it wasn't frightening even though my heart trembled − piles of soft flour-sacks, squashed one on the other, the curves smoothly bulging. The tram came clanging joyfully down the street, brightly-lit and almost empty, as we conversed like grown-ups, chatting away about all manner of things.

What did we say? What tales were they that gripped and grabbed and stirred us so?

The serenity of the youthful spirit which still overwhelms me and shafts me with longing. The serenity which has been my life's quest; I find it and it is gone, always gone again.

Her gaze dwelt long and musing. What was I saying? That special womanly gaze. Only men know what it means.

'Be easy, dear,' she said. 'You and your friend are the apples of my two eyes. But mind out, though. Lord be with you, Lord bless you. Me, Shenouda − the whole quarter knows. No one will dare go near you, dear. Our Lord bring you what you strive for and confound our country's enemies!'

What was she trying to say? Did they really all know? Did their concern for our safety really add up to secure, reliable protection?

I said nothing. Was my silence alone a betrayal? A confession?

The voice of the sheikh was lifted up in the Ramadan of my childhood, rippling out of the big wirelesses each with their single illuminated eye, from the shops and cafés and the open windows of houses before the evening cannon fired to break the fast. A voice which flowed like cool fresh water, beautiful, warning sadly of the punishments awaiting those who betray others and deny the Most Bountiful. Another Patriarch, yet he was himself, his voice fatherly, old and kindly, wearied by the burden of mercy to offenders, and even in the agony of faith accepting the rigorous descent of just chastisement. This emotion, this divine and compassionate grief which returns me once more to the streets of my childhood, my childhood hopes and scruples in Gheit el-Enab – worlds away now! Can I ever revivify those distant paradises of promise where the gates open to reveal the miracles within and shut fast in my face for all time? Those trees laden with pomegranates full of milk, honey and myrrh, the deep golden wine my father mixed with the water of his kindness and love and gave me to drink. I am an innocent child, the glass planes of flaring gas-lanterns are lit for us by a demon of the night with a long rod snapping sparks who passed on into the kingdom of the night whose boundaries we knew not. Where did he come from? Where did he go once he had left us our seeds of light, those quivering ripe fruits on the smooth dark dust of our streets – and where are they? The low house next to ours, just two storeys high, always closed up and strange but we knew that it was inhabited. We heard signs of life within but we never saw the people who lived there. The windows never opened to divulge its mysteries, it harboured always vast hidden still lakes within, the subjects of its kingdom, the bird-girls who shed their feathers to come to us once a year for they are the paradisal maidens whose beauty is unmatched in all lands. Where have the girls gone?

The power of these immanent memories. My heart is crushed by them.

All the horizons roamed by dreams where no man has set

foot, wide strands bordering càlm fresh waters where I have not been watered nor have I held back from drinking, seas my sails have not drifted over though my passions' gale itself blows them, cobbled streets of enchanted villages nestling between green meadows on the slopes of mountain valleys, pasturelands run through by brooks and channels of fresh clear water where massive columns lie riven the great cragged stones vigorously overgrown by fresh spring grass which thrives a scant few days, ruins uneffaced for time cannot break them. My soul brims over and yet is not quenched by a love which leaves me utterly bewildered, me and you, my beloved, also.

The rain drummed against the shutters. Carved lattice-like shutters. On and on, monotonous, for six days now.

The posh streets of Raml, the Royal Stadium district and the Greek quarter were clean and shining. The water babbled happily as it rushed away. As for the lanes I waded through on my way to the old quarter of Bahari and then to our house in Gheit el-Enab, these had become swamps of sticky evil-looking mud.

Fluid marble pulsing with the carnal clamour of the flesh, columns swayed by rocks, cushioned by the darkness of the obdurate heart, the thickness of bodily juices oozing from the ancient fissure of love and the marmoreal capitals crowned by stony sprays of vine, watered by grape wine laid down for ever and never broached; turning their face in silence to the horizon, questioning it in silence, edifices defying the years, the ages, the aeons and the earthquake of denial does not submit to them. My soul is broken in pieces with you on the round staircase of black marble, you stumble entangled in the stout threads of rejection's invisible net your arm is thin in my clasp a leafy bough fine-boned as it is always in my dream my hand never once closed about it though all through life it was no stranger to me, the daring needed to bring your arm and my hand together, the dream is the one truth in my eyes and the dream did not happen at all leave me leave me your face a fruit suffused with the blood of courage was it also the blood of the dream not one drop of which was shed the juices of rage pent up blow capture to the winds their bitterness is unbearable my fingers alone without my willing it brush a lock of hair from your shining temple the feel of a tumbling tress, the rush of blood in the open veins of desire until now my hand is a fragile leaf cast down by winter mornings whose fingers clutch upon a locked sky I refute it and nothing dies in the fall of darkness save the light surrounding the ruptured marble of your face and your body rising in ample plenitude in spite of the dereliction of the rites of violation and the founding of faith time after time without end in the morning and in the evening and your voice a benefaction and a sacrifice.

Three years before I did not know how my father would die suddenly on a bitterly cold night in December, nor how all sources of income would suddenly dry up, nor that hunger was a literally daunting tangible thing. I did not know how I would struggle by, teaching small children in their homes, the English ABC and the basics of arithmetic; how I'd go knocking on doors, how I'd write job application letters in search of a crust for me, my mother and my four sisters, or how later I would work – though it stuck in my craw to do it – for the English whose soldiery, whose obscene presence in our country in 1942 I loathed. I was still at the beginning of my university studies, I fancied myself a poet, a lover, I was in love with Norice Fakhry, Norice of the splendid magnificent bosom, and I was dying of bitterness and passion in murky solitude in her secret bliss without saying one word to anyone. I was romantic, I knew Shelley and Keats, Nagy and Ibn Zaydun, but of the dragon I knew only its gleaming yellow gold in the heart of my visions of a far-off faceless future. Oh – and my father brought me a white sharkskin suit whose rippling silken brilliance draped fluidly over me, and a red spotted tie and a pair of two-tone shoes, white on brown, with soft thick comfortable crêpe heels which squashed down a bit when I took a step the way a camel's foot did. And I didn't know how he would die at the end of the year.

Rommel had advanced as far as el-Alamein but we had become sick of fleeing to Akhmim or Damanhur or Tarrana. We'll stay in Alexandria and have done with it, we said, whatever the danger; the Lord is great. I loathed the Germans as I did the English. Let them go to Hell together, I said. At sixteen I was a conscious liberal, a vegetarian and an admirer of Rousseau and Qusayri and the surrealists. I wasn't overly concerned with the more momentous events of the first half of the twentieth century. But I did grieve at the fall of Paris which I had come to love from reading the works of Anatole France, Zaki Mubarak, Muhammad Sawi Muhammad and de Maupassant. I used to dream that I lived there in the essence of knowledge and freedom although I never knew the city at all — or rather only as an enamoured visitor of mature years elegizing his boyhood dreams.

The English had moved out of the Mustafa Pasha barracks leaving only a symbolic force behind. Smoke no longer rose from the chimneys of the British Consulate which stood like a fortress on a high hill opposite Raml Station, just before the Government hospital.

But the ATS girls still strode jauntily along the deserted Corniche in their bright white blouses, smart little ties and navy-blue skirts tight across their neat bottoms. They used to go down the short flight of steps and across the clean bare sands to the huts reserved for them on Mustafa Pasha beach. The huts were guarded by an armed picket who prevented us from so much as approaching the iron fence criss-crossed with barbed wire. The guards wore red berets and the red arm-bands bearing the letter MP in white. Wordlessly they waved their small pistols at us, insolent and cold, but we still managed to catch a glimpse of the tall slim-built white bodies in the dark costumes which were regulation issue from the army, navy or airforce stores. Shining in the Alexandrian winter noonday sun, they plunged into the breaking waves – there was always surf, just here. My friend Ahmad Sabri the artist invited me to spend the late afternoon at his family's summerhouse – their palace, to be truthful – out at el-Amriya. They were of Turkish or Circassian origin and extremely rich; they owned a lot of land in el-Beheira and Upper Egypt. I alighted from the el-Amriya train which was full of soldiers returning to the front. The open freight-cars carried small tanks, iron-clad vehicles with long, thin-barrelled guns, and high-sided army lorries covered with black tarpaulins.

The English had pitched camp at el-Amriya. The salt-lake rippled with a leaden reddish glitter under the afternoon light. Mirage castles glimmered on the skyline, seemingly built on the clouds, back-lit by the pale ancient gold of the sun. Little white tents were pitched row upon row far out into the desert over the high sandy ground beyond the railway tracks. No fences surrounded them, no guards, nothing. There were soldiers outside the tents, lying on camp-beds quietly reading their books and magazines in the bright daylight, or stripped to the waist and shaving – perhaps just to pass the time – with the aid of hand-mirrors, or simply stretched out and gazing idly at the sky. A lad my age or younger turned towards me. He gave my shiny white sharkskin suit and carefully-whitened crêpe-soled shoes a slightly mocking, contemptuous, envious stare, or so it seemed to me – as someone who had travelled far with no certain return might look upon the idle settled life of home. Now that the train had pulled slowly out a sudden afternoon calm reigned everywhere, a silence only emphasized by the few faint shouts of the soldiers across the empty space, the gusts of salty breeze rippling the surface of the great salt-lake. Although I was aware that the greater part of these boys were going to face imminent death, and that they themselves knew that they were children of death, I could not lift my hand in a silent salute which I believed in spite of everything to be their right. Didn't I say that I was romantic, that I had the heart of a boy still?

A short distance away on the other side of the tracks were the bedouin tents. They were black with low flaps, made of dark shaggy matted goatskins, and they gaped at the corners and at the guy-rope moorings where a thin cord stretched between tent and peg. Some short-legged but big-humped camels had paused to chew the cud by the remains of hearths where the embers still glowed and steam rose from the black bulbous cooking pots propped on top. Goats roamed nibbling at the dry thorny scrub. There was no one.

That night I spent in my friend Ahmad Sabri's palace. We returned the following day in the family Packard driven by a chauffeur in uniform and peaked cap. As we skirted the camp I saw rows of large lorries, abandoned and veiled in desert dust. The headlights were broken, the windows covered with cardboard, and the number-plates blacked out. Next to them were some small yellow armoured vehicles leaning over on their sides. The glass of the narrow horizontal slits in the front was black-looking and gleaming with the scattered reflections of the sun's rays, the metal tracks snapped and slack upon the ground. Some of the machines were covered in green camouflage netting. For the first time I noticed the guns, mounted on square concrete emplacements, the barrels stopped either by clinging sleeve-like coverings or tight round rubber caps or black waxed cloth glistening with grease. Wooden crates stood next to them in orderly stacks with big black letters and numbers painted on to the bare wood.

And we went back – as I never tire of going back – to Alexandria.

Shore of Alexandria O shore of passion
People of Alexandria we are felled by passion
Shore of Alexandria . . .

I deal in imaginings which take on the face of memories I turn
away from reality yet I seem to endure reality but obtain only
the body of the dream my encounters with the dream are
without number and they flit one and all from my craving grasp
what is the worth of tears shed for all the grieving and oppressed
both living and unrecompensed dead and then there is a romantic inverted longing for death a belief in it along with welcom-
ing expectancy nay a summons for it to come very near round
the next corner yearnings for eternity sharp teeth snapping
at the throbbing flesh no laxity there and ropes of jasper
cornelian coral wind about thighs and calves and basilican asps
and eels and spotted lynxes computer screens electrified by
flickering numbers by the million letters no one can read mercy
and love are vain in the vast sea where planet earth is floating
the bursting torrent which carries before it eyes penises wombs
split open and castrated amputated limbs the cuckoo screeches
in the slopes of the bared buttocks slipping between bramble-
thorns playing the violin the body vegetable slivers entwining
silken spiderlegs winding drinking of the rich black milk which
makes the engines of juggernauts roar on their undeviating way
what is new while the bloodshed rings out a long echo to no
avail in this wide sea which time and time again is beaten by
the moon's wane and the drought then ebbs and flows with the
flood-tide when it rushes into the interior in the world of
the body rent and gored delirium of lily of the valley quagmires
acrid filling the mouths of thirsty apes deformities of strict
design intoxicated convulsions glories of the hosanna and lauds
to the flesh yearning for the kingdom bosoms nestle brimming
over the fine pointed lace and lattice shutters gnawed by the
fangs of geckos and weasels slinking among fields of cotton and
maize and over the dust of the sleeping lanes where bare feet
sink the gazelle eternally fallen and bleeding eyes open unblinking lips dyed with the crimson blood of fallen prey which is
not watered and after the succession of dreams tumbling only
to rise again one by one strips of flesh shredded stretched out on

the milestones of the road comes fear no stark terror carefully-concealed from that inner enemy killer who lives now within the fastness of your ribs black elder not for the stranger as I said I am a stranger I do not know how to reach my womb where is my womb? I do not know them the breach in the red sycamore tree bared to his blood open for ever the chill plunge into the world of the embryo between blue and blush the heart a yellow pigeon the shiny black glass it is the traveller's trudge over the summits of skyscrapers above the coast at Sidi Bishr where degradation is permitted the clinging vine winds and tightens its noose squeezing the waists which overflow on to the rolling dunes and love in this high sea flows and ebbs in desire in lust in the feel of longing for the other body for the hectic cleaving in search of deliverance from this suppression which is compulsory white Coca-Cola froth bathes the burning but does not extinguish the hot breaths when they blow flaring panting upon the undefended fortresses of aroused sensation incense of sapinwood of cinnamon of red myrrh of white markings wafting in the sightless gorges in ever-imperfect rings unflaggingly echoing with desire to the end the beginning without beginning or end interior conflagration the salamander burns in the fire and water hits the serpent milk floods from its open mouth not in invitation but always now. Metaphysics of flesh defying incarnation, defying answers.

It was eight o'clock on a wintry Friday morning. I had come early to see my friend Qasim Ishaq at the house in Bahari. I did not find him there. I hammered on the door of his roof-flat but there was no reply. My heart sank. Suppose the police had got him at last? What could I do now?

Baby Mikha'il's mother opened her door below. 'Effendi! Effendi!' she called. 'Your friend left yesterday.'

'Left – what? Just like that? Was he on his own?'

'Calm down a minute, do. No, it's just the men in the

130

building went with him as far as the beginning of *shari'* No. 15. Shenouda carried his bag for him all the way to the tram-stop. They stayed with him until he got on the tram.'

I suddenly imagined the pressures on the owner of the build-ing. Somehow or other he had been compelled to go back on his agreement with us and forego the precious five pounds' rent for the roof-flat: 'No offence, sir, effendi! Blessings on him who is perfect light! Mercy on the Prophet! I mean, we're good Egyptians too, we know what's right. We have the highest regard for you both, really we do. But you know, the spirit's willing, but . . . I leave it to your discretion. And there are women in the house . . . well, things may get a bit complicated. It's just that women, you know . . . and we're good Arabs, we're hot-blooded. We can't put up with students around the house all the time. Young men, I mean, alone in the house with the women. Not one of us any better than the next. All trying to get by. And that's hard, effendi, sir. And honour is hard as well. No offence – I mean we won't say anything. God forbid – dear God, the idea that we should ever! . . . You can depend on us. You're both fine well-brought-up young men, I knew that at first sight. But you see when it comes to my reputation I just can't. And the people in the quarter have made us feel this small. You can trust a villain to get the upper hand. You know best of anyone. Each and every person here by the life of Sidi'l Mursi said, This has gone far enough. Listen though, sir. The men can easily take you to a safe place as well . . .'

As she said goodbye to me for the last time I suddenly noticed the faded blue of the tattoo she had, the foliate Coptic cross on the inside of her smooth brown wrist.

The baby was in her arms, just like the first time. But her breast was in the mouth of the serpent.

The serpent was huge. Its broad wings were spread out motionless in the air. It leaped easily from the top of the wooden spiral staircase beneath the courtyard window. The wings hardly fluttered. It alighted on the top of the ancient palm which stood alone in the dusty gloom of the yard.

My features were imprinted on the pupils of its glassy eyes.

Did I kill its peerless intimate who rises living still – and did I only want to kill her or did I really do it – and comes tirelessly back again, back again?

Can she ever die?

8

A Gazelle Brought Down on the Sand

My friend Antoine discovered unexpectedly that he had tuberculosis.

Unable to shake off a cough which had dragged on all winter, he went to the doctor. When the doctor X-rayed his chest he found that Antoine had a small 'patch' on his left lung.

In the summer I received a letter from him, from the Lebanon, in painstakingly clear and absolutely faultless French.

> *My dear friend,*
>
> *I am sorry that I have taken so long to write to you. The condition of my nerves and spirit has so far prevented me from doing so. I cannot elaborate since writing – and reading – quickly tire me out.*
>
> *My health is a little better than it was in Alexandria. Unfortunately I am assailed from time to time by a nervous depression which robs me of what little weight I have gained over these long weeks of patience.*
>
> *To escape the past and the present I have but two alternatives: either to rummage through my stock of ghostly childhood memories, thereby casting myself into a slough of despond and profound sorrow; or to watch the minutes, hours, days creep past without doing anything at all, which is the cause of my stagnant and morose depression.*

I console myself with the thought that I will soon be with you all in Alexandria – and especially with you, my dear friend.

I hope that you are not visited too often by your own melancholies. I hope also that you will write me a long letter (in Arabic, if you prefer, or in English). Not only will it cheer me, but it will go some way to appease my hunger to see you again.

My fond regards to all our friends and two big kisses to N. Tell her I miss her a great deal and write to me with her news. Kiss Umm Dawlat for me as well, and ask her if she has finished writing her memoirs!

I send you a thousand kisses and the warmest of embraces.

Please don't ask about my health when you write. I will tell you why later.

My address is: C/O al-Khawaja Shukri Dahir, Rummana'l Ghaba.

I was already impervious to the tone of youthful ardour which dominated his letter. I had received my first taste of it years before, from my friend Shafiq Pastroudis Raqim, and I had been swayed by it then. In 1942 we had both been forced to leave Alexandria; I went with my mother and sisters to Akhmim, Shafiq to his family home in Saft el-Muluk where his father was the station-master. During this period we wrote one another what amounted to love letters. Disappointment was inevitable when it became clear after a short time how shallow this tone was in spite of its heat, how artificial, and afterwards I told him that he had been false even in his representation of facts. This created a breach I made no move to heal, especially since he later let me down completely in a crisis – and perhaps I had to do the same to him, who knows. Although we managed nevertheless to sustain a lifelong friendship I always sensed a caution on both sides which was only natural in the circumstances.

And circumstances had their capricious way with us. He travelled to London, settling there permanently after his heart attack. He loathed Egypt because she had accepted Nasser, glorified him and made him a god; he loathed her because she had rejected Nasser, sullied his name and condemned him. He hated her people for their apathy, their backwardness, corruption and squalor; he wished them all dead. His wife told me that when he was alone in his room he cried with love and longing for Egypt. When I visited him last year in his exile I realized beyond doubt that we had become two worn-out old men and I felt time gnawing at my heart. He had all the prejudices of an old man; he had the lips of an old man too, pursed over false teeth, and his vague eyes were fixed permanently on an imagined and utterly unreal future. Of the wondrous, marvellous youth of the forties there was nothing left except a too-tight jacket – that, and a presumed superiority to the world which stemmed from being sheltered from the same. I still hold him dear. There is no one who can take his place in my heart.

But what really rather vexed me in Antoine's letter was his way of talking about himself – and about my girl Ni'ma. It is strange, but I have completely forgotten whether Umm Dawlat was writing her memoirs, although I have not forgotten the love letters she wrote in the style of cheap novels.

Antoine did not know that I was seeing his sister Odette. Perhaps he merely pretended not to know. Certainly he knew that I visited the family house behind the Ladies' Alley in el-Manshiya el-Sughayara whether he was there or not, and that it was Odette whom they called to receive and entertain me. I had the feeling that her parents and her sister Arlette looked on me as something approaching a fiancé in spite of the pains I took to avoid being seen in that light or giving the barest intimation of such intentions. Nevertheless I didn't categorically refute these casual and delicate allusions when they were tossed, as they usually were, into the conversation. Would it have been possible openly to refute them, to risk such rupture and alienation? I do not know.

At that time I loved with a love from which I could not, did not want to be delivered, which I was none the less unable to attain.

Years later I married. I came to Cairo and lost all contact with Odette. I knew only that she had not married. How did I know that? I cannot remember. Once I was in the Souq el-Tawila in Beirut when suddenly I found myself face to face with her. We both stopped and stared at each other, neither saying a word. She simply looked at me, and I shall never forget that look. She had aged, her face was lined; it was a broken woman I saw before me, one who had done battle against time and despair. Then she turned on her heel and walked away. I never saw her again and made no effort to inquire about her. Where is she now? How is she?

I deserve it, this hardheartedness. I don't deny that I am worthy of it.

But in my enduring juvenile *naïveté* I cannot accept, not even now, this harshness which is inevitable, even necessary, in life. No. I cannot condone it.

I said: Why this tireless agonizing over what is past and gone? This querulous investigation into vanished lives?

I said: Is it because the quest for immortality – permanence at least – is the foundation of your Romanticism, of its unde-molished rock-foundation?

And I said: Joining and sundering, meeting and parting, death and life – all these and all pertaining to them are accidental, they are contingent, they are lawless. Or rather that is their law; the law of transience and cease.

I asked: And the threads that bind your life, are they naught but torn and severed shreds dangling in the void?

I replied: That is not so. These things are not fated but willed. They are acts occurring essentially from free will.

I said: Then what is the problem?

In that summer of the early fifties my friend Antoine came

back from the Lebanon. His doctor had advised him to spend two weeks in a calm, dry, clear atmosphere.

He reserved a room in a small hotel called 'Mon Repos', taking another for me without saying anything at the time and then pressing me to take some time off and come with him – to drive away the miseries and horrors of his depression, as he put it.

I was with him in his office at the Messageries Maritimes Company when he dialled el-Amriya 23, confirmed the reservation and learned the price for a room and three meals. (It was a hundred and forty piastres – fifteen for breakfast, forty for lunch, forty-five for supper and forty for the room). To reach the hotel, he discovered, we had to take the Alexandria – el-Amriya bus, number 15 from Raml Station. He had not bought his car yet, the second-hand Citroën we once drove to Cairo along the desert road, taking two hours less five minutes to reach Giza Square which still looked like a village then.

'Just you be careful of the TB, my boy,' said my mother. 'We've only got you. He, now, he's got his father and brothers, God preserve them, all earning nicely. But who have we got apart from you and the good Lord?'

She knew that there was no point trying to dissuade me.

'There's nothing for you to worry about,' I said.

'Let the Guardian of Israel, Who sleeps not and misses nothing, keep you safe!' she said.

'Enough about Israel!' I replied, laughing and angry at once.

She did not understand why I laughed, or why I was angry.

We alighted from the half-empty bus at sunset on Saturday evening. The few Bedouin in hooded gowns, open waistcoats, long narrow drawers all made of the same yellowish-white material, the women in their heavy costumes, the heavy tattoos on their chins, the heavy kohl around their eyes, their heavy jangling jewellery, and it was they and not the men who humped and tossed down the bundles, the packs, the baskets and the burdens – these Bedouin had alighted from the bus at places far from any visible stop. One of them shouted, 'Stop, driver, stop!' and the driver obediently and silently stopped as if he also knew the different sites and routes even though these shifted, changing according to season and conditions.

I knew this small hotel. There was a time when I came regularly to spend the entire day here, returning only in the late afternoon. In that season sportsmen after sparrows, thrushes and quail would come for the weekend, rising at dawn to spray shot from the long shining barrels of their guns into the bushy trees of the spreading hotel park.

I had come once on a company excursion. Philippe Nakhla was part of the group along with his Yugoslavian fiancée Janine Birkowitz, his friend Thomas – pasty Thomas with the little paunch – my friend Selim Andrawos, Yvette Sassoon, Su'ad el-Samahi, Madeleine and her sister Miryam, plus Stepho, Yvonne and Maria. We took the traditional snaps, later sold to us by the company public relations department at half the cost price, which capture us staring at the camera in a moment of shiny-papered immortality. We rode little desert donkeys Happy Festivities to you Monsieur and you Madame all around the hotel grounds and the park for two piastres the half-hour, expensive but what does it matter today we're fancy free; the donkey's jutting bones hurt me and I suspected fleas carried hidden in the thick saddle padded with old blankets and in the colourful striped woollen wraps. We swung on swings – I could see the hotel roof as I went up, rough stone falling away below me as I rose until I touched the sky, before the roof rose in turn, and the debris of stone and wood appeared for the first time beneath the kitchen walls as the smoke rose slowly from the tall black iron chimney. We stole bunches of grapes which weren't quite ripe, munching them well out of sight of Madame Ulrike who would still give us doubtful anxious looks when we returned with innocent eyes and spotless hands. We played hide and seek on condition that we did not go into the drawing-room or the bedrooms and only ran about and hid behind the wall or amongst the trees, irrigation canals and vineyards.

Amm Bashir came to the door to welcome us. He was an old, spare, upright Nubian in a large white turban and long grey woollen robe. Now that night had fallen the air was beginning to cool, though the heat of the day was still borne on the desert breeze.

I noticed an open jeep speeding away from the back gate of the hotel. It crunched over the gravelled track, stirring up clouds of dust mingled with flying scraps of dead leaves. The harsh whine of the engine violated the desert's tranquil silence. I also saw the back of a black leather jacket slung negligently over a strong athletic back, a collar unbuttoned at a stout neck, a thick black Stalin moustache and a gaunt dark profile. Beside him, sitting very close on the uncovered leather seat, was a white-skinned, fine-featured youth. And soon I saw the long line of sand swirling under the powerful wheels as they ploughed over the tract of desert.

'That's Mursi Bey and his friend Hammuda,' said 'Amm Bashir. 'They're going to find out where the gazelle sleeps.'

I found this remark a bit odd. Although I didn't fully understand what he said I didn't ask him to explain.

A tiny impish boy by the name of Farag appeared. He heaved the two big bags together on to his shoulder and, lopsided under the weight, took the third bag in his arm. He and the luggage, now fairly amalgamated into one lumpen creature of three interconnecting segments, moved energetically away.

The little hotel – just eleven rooms and a ground floor – had a verandah overlooking the desert. It was protected by a screen of hinged oblong panes of thick glass. We sat there drinking tea after the evening meal, the desert night lying dark before us. I could sense it stretching far, far away over the sand, glimmering with small yellow blinking filaments of light like tiny shining pin-pricks; I could not determine where or what they were. At nightfall the desert was an utterly lonely place.

139

The only sound came from the big old-fashioned wireless as it whispered in the drawing-room inside, its single round electric eye glowing in the gloom. Almost inaudible, it made the silence heavier.

Madame Ulrike, the Swiss-born owner of the hotel, was listening to the wireless. A fair, petite, dainty figure, she sat curled up in the big flowery cretonne armchair. There was a little table at her side covered in old illustrated magazines, *Images* and *Illustrations*, and English and French detective stories in yellow covers.

It was during our last visit that Madame Ulrike had told us how she came to Egypt with her husband in the 'Great War'. He had chosen this lonely spot in the middle of the desert's vastness to dig an artesian well driven by a large windmill. He planted the park to the rear of the hotel before he was killed by an old landmine when hunting out in the desert. Madame Ulrike said that she had made up her mind to stay and take care of the park, which had flourished to its present profusion under her hands.

We could feel it out there in the night, dark and thick with the trunks of fig trees grown and gnarled now, with murky olive trees, with Christ's thorn, sycamore and mulberry trees. And beyond the glass screen, the pure, open virgin sands.

We kept silence. Untouched by any sense of isolation or banishment, we gave ourselves up to the desert's omnipotent mystery.

By the light of high lamps shining down outside the balcony on to the sand we spotted grey fat-bellied desert rats scuttling across in front of us on their special paths. A small fox came towards the screen, pausing not far away, separated from us by the thick glass. Its eyes flashed with a cold electric glow, its ears were taut and pricked in a mixture of discovery, apprehension and curiosity. The thick bushy tail bristled upright, poised to quiver, almost as long as the creature's shy, wild body. One moment – and then a sudden fright or pressing desire possessed it, and away it dashed into the familiar realm of night.

Mursi Bey came back, a wide-awake, tense air about him. His companion Hammuda however slumped slack-featured beside him. We exchanged perfunctory greetings. Antoine was clearly exhausted, so he went to bed while I sat on in silence until well past midnight.

Early the following morning, before a cup of milky tea, before breakfast was prepared, I went out with Antoine. We strolled for a while among the tangled greenery of the woodlands.

The water purling in the long irrigation channels glittered in a daybreak heralded by hidden throngs of birdsong. Sunlight glanced in a quivering shift of shadows cast by high, lilting casuarina trees on to ground half-sandy, half-veiled by sharp needle-like leaves. The little channels in the earth branched in all directions, along and across, filled by deep narrow wells sunk at regular intervals, deep and black and glassy and surrounded by stone walls. Ropes hung down inside, each with a bucket wrapped in wet canvas, the tough wiry threads stretched tightly over it. On the border of the park by the kitchen, the huge wheel of the great artesian well turned slowly in the gentle breeze.

Then, through the low dense coppices of short scaly palm trees, I caught a glimpse of two big eyes. Greenish eyes, it seemed to me in that fleeting glance; eyes with a strange look in them certainly, the look of a hunted creature, a mixture of craven fear and desperate courage. The pitch-black hair was caught in a thin faded blue ribbon which was the only indication that the creature was female. A skinny thing entirely, limber as a youth, a pretty thing in its way. But the thin legs in old narrow trousers cut off at the knee, the ancient, too-big pullover dusted with desert sand, the faded damp patch over a chest where the breasts were hardly discernible – all this gave her beauty a fey, untamed, animal quality.

141

The face, which had obviously been anxiously and yet hope-fully watching us, vanished.

I heard Amm Bashir's husky old man's voice calling from the kitchen, 'Rawiya! Rawiya, girl!'

Antoine's breathing had quickened – from the early exercise? From the sight of this extraordinary girl? Or was it in fact a convalescent's weakness? A dark flush had replaced the waxen pallor of his high jutting cheekbones.

He said simply, 'Wait'.

Rawiya – so that was her name – approached quickly now. She dashed along, slightly hunched, leaping fast over the ditches and the unexpected clumps of reeds, skirting the wiry young fig trees and dodging the vines laden with massed juicy bunches of grapes. She was carrying half a piece of coarse flat bread and a round earthenware dish of yoghurt. I could still see her eyes, panic-stricken, staring, burning with hunger, anxiety and terror, like a desert rat or a weasel slipping between sand and green towards the outer wall of the kitchen. The voice, carrying strains of feebleness and resignation, called on. 'Rawiya! Rawiya!' The expanse of desert echoed with the sharp call but it was almost lost in the thick foliage of the gardens. The rubble by the stone wall of the kitchen, the old and new logs where some were charred, the high ash-heap and the debris of doused fires: all this gave the place a disquieting air. It flashed through my mind: Was she – disgraceful, shameful idea – exploited sexually as well? Was this childish, boyish body fair game?

With slow deliberation Amm Bashir laid before us dishes of fried eggs with shiny yellow yolks and a mouthwatering aroma, sour cheese as white as milk, and soft-skinned green and black Greek olives.

'Mursi Bey and his friend have found out where the gazelle sleeps,' he said.

'Amm Bashir,' I asked suddenly, idly. 'Who's the new girl who works with you?'

He made no reply. He did not seem to have heard.

'The girl,' I repeated. 'The one you were calling this morning. The one called Rawiya. Where's she from?'

Avoiding my gaze he turned away and left us without a word. I thought little of it. He's old now, I said, and a bit woolly-minded.

The rumble of ancient glories still echoes, the dust of ancient battles still whirls, and your face still shines out in desert gorge and desert fold the telegraph poles grow wider apart the wires strung and dipping slack from tip to tip have vanished behind hillocks of pebbles multicoloured or dark or veiled with a layer of smooth sand the world is forsaken and the jeep with its strong metal sides shines and dips down into silent troughs where now there is no shade but rather perfect brilliance perfect mystery and the hunted creature rises and falls far off slender columns lithe living boughs playing the music of desperation holding fast against despair the flame of the sun a heart open to the limit thick rubber wheels grind into it in final resolution a spring without water a furious repressed sea afire with ancient griefs sharp-toothed time has deceived us time has run out our pouch is emptied of treasures and slipped our hands a void of time there is no drop of water and fire is latent beneath a layer of pebbles and coarse sand wide rings of the hum of the chase while the silence of flight is enchanted no breeze within the emptiness of a hollowed eggshell of boundless size the sun of Joshua stops in her heart to beat but not split and the noon of the last hour does not end my love is a desert and a sheet of lead burning on sightless lightless the jeep still runs rings about the prey afloat on the music of her imminent fall and dashes her to the ground the horizon bears no echo of the call always water soundless brine a shore renewed again no depth there no sea no end to the blue salt a call froth hollowing cinema seats torn out and lifeless in my hand scattered like seedcorn white peeled kernel and what is it that burns with futile fire? thin

143

columns of fragile bone or stripped boughs dishevelled locks singe with the odour of charrred flesh we are naked we are free of time we have passed beyond the last point the jeep approaches savage deliberate the wide-eyed prey we are now in the zone of the gratuitous we have broken the boundaries no account for anything anyone breaths come quick pant pant pant the rhythm rigid unabating but the rapacity of the sands fix on it the fall of the thin body plummetting echoless to the ground the eyes staring the look of terror a hunted creature still ultimate terror the call is a screaming blue the gunshot once then again it is ugly the way she collapses it is ugly the growl of the engine.

I had awoken from a troubled uneasy afternoon sleep under the whine of the big ceiling fan which increased the heat in the room by stirring the hot air around. I saw the jeep coming through the gate in the wall of the garden at the back. Amm Bashir and the boy Farag went running out to it. Did I see the gazelle, slain and tied by a rope in the back of the jeep, head hanging, legs bunched together? And did I see – for a moment I could not believe my eyes, and then the jeep vanished – a thin body in the back seat, a thin ribbon circling the head stained blackish-red with dried wetness? A body also limp, ravished for the last time and tossed aside, oddly slack?

When we came out for our afternoon cup of tea the gazelle was lying on the sand. The bullet blast had left a rough ragged hole in the middle of the back of the skull. Its eyes were still open, the fixed vitality in them defying the hunt, refusing the end.

I could not bear it. Amm Bashir had a long thin knife in his hand. He was slitting the soft pale brown hide and starting to skin the gazelle in preparation for roasting. I went for a long walk over the sand, alone, without thinking of anything in particular.

144

At the time when I was learning pre-Islamic poetry by heart and translating a novel called *The Black Arrow*, and I was in love with the aristocratic maiden, the one with the blue silk robe who appeared on the balcony opposite our house and then went inside again on her way to the walled garden where mango and banana trees rose behind the villa – at this time I used to go to the Abbasiya Secondary School, where I was in the second year, via a short cut through the middle of Muharram Bey.

The clean gravelly sandy street led me up the hill. I slipped through a hole in the old thick wall made of rubble and cement, where the rough surface had turned an ashy yellow, to find myself on the slope of a sandy hillock. A gentle slope, firm underfoot where I was assailed by the smell of sheep, goats and camels, their dung and wool and hides, where there were dark dusty felt tents torn and re-sewn time and again, I could see, with scraps of leather patching the repairs. Low tents, dark inside, scattered over the hillside among the few thin high-grown palms. The bleating of the goats rose with the hearth smoke.

On Fridays when my mother went to market and left me at home I gathered around me my sisters Aida and Hana, my African-faced cousin Maria, and Iskandara my first cousin once removed. In my most ringing tones I recited all the poems I had by heart, the tales of Arabia before Islam with their rhythmic beat, their eloquent clangour. Brandishing my arms about I recited, without fudging or skipping so much as a word, and the girls listened to me rapt, horrified, marvelling. I chanted the poetry of Ibn Abi Rabi'a and Qais who was called The Mad, and I would forget myself, my voice trembled nigh-weeping, and I saw the girls look at me with welling eyes . . .

The bedouin camp would be quiet when I came out at exactly a quarter to seven, my textbooks and jotters in my arms. The girls followed their flocks of goats out into the calm of *shari'* Muharram Bey where the beasts grazed on scraps of newspaper, leaves or old rags. Suddenly I would be in Arabia, in Najd or Tihama or the Hejaz, astride the she-camel of Qais with the little bedouin girl huddled in her striped robe, her nose pierced with a serrated gold ring and her hair hidden under a wide red scarf, hidden save for two plaits braided with colourful grubby-looking ribbon. But her black eyes gleamed with passion in a golden-brown face oval beneath the opaque half-veil covering her mouth – I never glimpsed her lips, I never knew her smile – and she was looking at me. I loved her very much. I called her Fanstasmal Layla. I passed on slowly beneath the brow of the hill.

She came lilting down, her firm close-pressed buttocks moving rhythmic and supple beneath the wide red sash binding her belly. Gone were the few low houses surrounding the camp at a distance, gone was the braying of an old camel resounding harsh and choked in this throat. Gone was the campfire smoke in my nose. I was aware only of the courtly lovers, I learned of Jamil lover of Buthayna and Azza beloved of Kuthayir and Qais the Mad, all dwelling in this heart which was – and even in maturity still is – yearning, craving, brimming with love and with the dream.

I left the dusty dirt square beneath the hill as if I were leaving an enchanted world, a place of rags and tatters and mixed provenance, a narrow, rugged downward path. I found myself once more on the wide tarmacked street, home of the Lady Cromer Clinic where my mother brought me when I was very young to have the Englishwoman swab my eyes; home also of Amm Subhi's shop which I visited every single day before going to the Abbasiya School. He sold lupine seeds, peanuts and chick peas, exercise books, blue paper for covering textbooks, and little white labels edged with blue curlicues. And, most important of all, he lent out magazines and paperbacks, first for two milliemes and later for two-and-a-half, and this second coin was a five-sided nickel one bearing the image of the young Farouq in the *tarboosh* and high buttoned collar of ceremonial dress. At the beginning of the year I had paid Amm Subhi half a piastre as a deposit, in case I lost a book or got so mad about it that I decided not to give it back. I devoured them at night when everyone was asleep, waiting eagerly to turn back the covers illustrated with faces in dramatic hues or beautiful ladies in long evening dresses slit at the long, gleaming rosy thigh. *Nana, La Dame aux Camelias, Sappho* with the face of Greta Garbo, *The Blue Angel* with the face of Marlene Dietrich, *Anna Karenina, Paul et Virginie.* The girls of Mahmud Kamil, aristocratic girls at the wheel of automobiles in Maadi, the Pyramids Road, Zamalek – all of them enchanted places for me – or chatting on the telephone to lovers in the still of the night – and the telephone as well was an instrument of magic to me. How many hot tears I shed, streaming tears convulsing my entire body, in the inmost core of a heart awakening agitated from troubled childhood into turbulent adolescence. My mother kept pigeons in the loft and their monotonous cooing filled the near-empty rooms whenever they were woken at night by the light from my bedroom. My father had no work and we were selling the furniture or pawning it and redeeming it later; sometimes the bed would be gone, at other times the bureau or the set of dining-room chairs, and then back they would come. No mats or carpets covered the floor, especially in the summer, and the pigeons fluttered down on to the tiles and strutted about the house pecking for seeds and crumbs and leaving their little greenish-white dropping behind them. When the droppings dried my mother swept them up and piled them in the loft. She called down to the man who went through the streets crying 'Pigeon droppings' and sold this hard dry peculiar-smelling excrement. The fat spotted marmalade cat prowled through the rooms mewing and sniffing at the floor, not daring to approach the big pigeons with particoloured feathers and puffed chests whose cooing dwindled and then raced loud

147

and inimical as I sat reading beneath the window opposite the balcony belonging to the girl in the blue robe. I read Rider Haggard and Walter Scott in English, books in thick red dust-covers borrowed from the school library. I loved the feel of those books and I still do. How I was gripped by *Aisha* and *She!* How I searched for the treasure of King Solomon in the Mountains of the Moon! How my heart pounded along with the cannons of the Caribbean corsairs!

The inundating flood of waves which did not bear away my vessel am I still a child with no heaven and the world a monster reborn and I have not trodden the paths of the Mountains of the Moon and there is exile in the deep eyes which did not look at me once a lover's looks parch the moist hidden places of wounds the friction of greedy roughness with warm silken softness the world is torn down slowly the braying of the old camel unwilling to kneel while the beast is near raising his head again again have you not done singing of the perfidious bosom? the blue sky ripples hotly over the slithering body and the cool moisture in the open depth a wound ever unhealed the waters gush in a rough babble I travel amongst the ruins of the heavens these fangs and blows of the monsters feet thumping the ground dead again again the pain afresh newborn intolerable scorch of the breath of inexplicable desire the code ever uncracked the thirst ever unquenched the bowels filled with the customary agony the body cannot emerge from the stupor the frenzy which seems foreign to it and there is nothing more intimate than this fragile ecstasy without horizon tiny stabwounds seeming coral beads of blood oozing near-transparent in the roundness of their seeds the pangs of my passions neither run dry nor heal the sun glints on the quivering pomegranates full and crimson the tremor in the hidden darkened troughs the fever of lust is a blow a gunshot it is fatal it cannot be thwarted.

Antoine was reclining on the upholstered chaise-longue on the balcony. The thick glass panes had been opened to admit the refreshing late afternoon breeze. He looked defeated, flung on the sand, stubborn; as pallid as if all his blood had been drained away. I felt a tremor of fear for him. As if he had read my thoughts, he gave me a brave wan smile.

'Don't worry,' he said. 'Rascals live longest.'

Years later I visited him in Ashrafiya, in Beirut. He had the usual type of bourgeois apartment, full of all the smart knick-knacks we like to call 'antiques'. The building had a garden in the form of a small overgrown walkway. The Citroën sat in front of it, everything inside limited and confined and redolent of small-time success. Baldness had begun to encroach on the head of hair which in Alexandria had been so carefully tended and there was a lined, dry, strained, withdrawn look about his face. We had lunch *en famille* at the flat. His wife, whom he had known since they worked at SAS Airlines opposite the cinema in *shari'* Fuad, had let herself go a bit – she was pencil-slin in her day – and she only talked to me in French or Lebanese. She must have forgotten Egyptian Arabic; she had never spoken it very well, in any case, even when she was in Alexandria. His son and daughter, the regulation two point zero children, seemed as utterly foreign to me as I was to them. The boy, Robert, was engaged in memorizing aloud a patriotic Lebanese poem; he spoke about Camille Chamoun with a child's incomparable loyalty. (This was before the Civil War.) As for the girl, she refused to sit at the table with us, then burst into tears and was taken away by her mother into the inner rooms of the flat. Her mother whispered to her inaudibly, no doubt soothing the fear engendered by this stranger who spoke a strange and forgotten Alexandrian tongue. The stranger who I was.

The years, as they do, came between us. I do not know whether he is still alive or whether he died in the catastrophies of Beirut. I know that the turbulent desire to see him again which had surged in my heart was swept away by the circumstances of our respective lives. Whether I see him again or no, we will remain complete strangers to each other. Whether he still walks the earth or is gone from us there is no longer, really there is not, any bond between us at all. We sat at the table in his house hardly knowing what to say to one another, and I cannot believe my hardheartedness when I set down these chilly conjectures, hazarded guesses, suppositions and see them for themselves. During lunch I found that he sometimes forgot himself and slipped back into Lebanese, or had to search for an Egyptian word, and although I love the dialect on the tongues of the Lebanese a small part of my spirit shrivelled and died when I heard Antoine speak it.

Where did they go, the footsoldiers of the Alexandrian revolutionary circle of 1946? We used to meet Antoine at the Messageries Maritimes office in *shari'* Sesostris after working hours. The door was opened for us by Amm Saleh, the young Nubian porter who understood everything that went on and did not utter a word. On the French Roneo copier we printed out our pamphlets calling for evacuation, for the nationalization of the Suez Canal, for the defeat of subjugation, capitalist exploitation and underdevelopment; calling also for support to be given to the workers' strikes at the Bolvara factory and the spinning and weaving mills of Karmuz. Fattuh el-Qaffas typed them on to the silky transparent duplicating paper at the patent office owned by an old Maltese Jew, a paunchy man with a loud voice who emigrated to South Africa in 1948 leaving the office to his son-in-law. The son-in-law was obliged to go into partnership with an Alexandrian lawyer from an old Wafd party family who joined first Nasser's liberation organization, then the Nationalist Union and finally the Socialist Union, and who managed to slip through the net of nationalization.

Amm Saleh calmly and silently helped us work the Roneo copier. There was never any doubt that he read the inflammatory headlines and saw the hammer and sickle and the number

4 at the top of the silken duplicating paper. After Antoine left and I lost touch with him and left Alexandria myself, I used to go to the Air France office wher Amm Saleh worked. He was an old man by then but still vigorous and upstanding. When I greeted him he always remembered me and greeted me in turn, enthusiastically and with love, and asked after all those who had gone, those of whom we knew nothing now.

We printed the pamphlets in semi-darkness so that we would not be given away by lights burning in the company after hours. I took half of them to Zaki Ibrahim Sadduq, a Jewish boy who was Egyptian born and bred, a pure Alexandrian, and who worked at the Bolvara factory. He lived down an alley in el-Attarin with his family; his sister Marcelle, his mother in her long gown and kerchief and his little father who earned a living by going from house to house mending chairs. Zaki limped a bit and his left arm was withered but he was as bright as a button, a fervent believer in the revolution and a fierce enemy of Zionism. As a boy he had worked in grocery stores and carriage stables, for blacksmiths and tinsmiths, but he was rewarded at last with a factory job. He wore a gown under a traditional Egyptian overcoat. He could just abaut write his name in Arabic, and knew not a word of any other language.

In 1949 King Farouq's police put him on a ship by force and sent him to Genoa.

We were coming out of the Messageries Maritimes office. I had the duplicating paper and half the bundle of pamphlets folded underneath my dark blue raincoat, the one I had taken with written permission signed and sealed by Mr Lee from the British Navy Depot at Kafr Ashri. It was in the pocket of this coat that I later hid the three old hand-grenades my friend Ahmad el-Nems had bought from the bedouin at el-Amriya. Ahmad el-Nems was an Islamic terrorist until I argued with him, lectured him, instructed him for many long weeks. Then he became a Marxist-Leninist, a Trotskyite who held unswervingly to his beliefs − even now, even after wandering through

151

a wilderness of exile teaching mathematics in Zaire and translating learned papers for the United Nations in Paris, Geneva and Vienna . . .

I came down from Abbasiya Hill – there was a university there now, Farouq I – after night had fallen. I crept down the steep slope always lush and green with grasses in tangled profusion.

We decided by an overwhelming majority to hold a sit-in. All the previous three days people had been throwing sandwiches and other dry food wrapped in napkins through the windows to us, right across *shari'* el-Iskandarani. The army, with their small tanks which looked like toys, surrounded us as we stood guard over the body of a martyr slain by an English bullet at Raml Station. We dug him a grave on the university campus and kept a candlelit vigil there. Huge candles; where did we find the candles? We took it in turns to give revolutionary speeches and sing patriotic hymns.

In the darkness of the verdant slope I was reasonably hidden. The tanks were a fair distance away. I passed quietly by in front of them and none of them turned towards me.

I entered an old house by way of a narrow darkened entrance hall. I almost lost my footing on two crumbled steps of the long dirt stairway on the other side of the house which led down to the slope of the potters' yard. For the front door was on street level while at the back this long flight of steps was dug out of the slope itself, and the place even now returns to me in my dreams. This route was known to only a few of our number.

The dusty sidestreets were empty and bleak, dead ends with a building at the bottom. Retracing my steps I turned down one of the gloomy alleys branching off the sidestreets where the mud-brick walls of the houses were blank and windowless. I dashed down, the momentum of my descent propelling me irreversibly onward, until I came out at the fire station. The short thick round columns resembled those of Gothic monasteries full of vaults and winding tunnels and paved passages where a little new grass sprouted between the cracks. The little yard was empty except for gravel and sand, and surrounded by enormous warehouses whose iron doors, running on wheels, were closed now beyond any hope. But there was a big gleaming brass bell hanging from a high tower on a stout rope, calm and motionless. I saw the big dark metal tongue of the bell. I thought that when this bell was rung everybody in the town would wake, indeed all the bells in Egypt from Alexandria to Shallalat would ring in once ceaseless tolling clamour loud enough to wake the dead. This was no church bell, it was a proper railway or fire-station bell. It was silent, heavy, untouched by so much as a tremor. It was surrounded by firemen who were stationed like guards, with yellow Roman-shaped helmets and full dark-blue firefighting gear.

There was a large dark patch on the sand. On the back of the jeep and the fat spare wheel fixed there I saw a sprinkling of dried blood.

Amm Bashir and Farag were stooped over the cuts of meat. They were cleaned now and carefully wiped. I saw the hide stretched out to dry on the washing line. The breeze had been blowing with its own fresh scent but suddenly the direction of the wind changed and brought with it an unbearable odour – the remnants of the entrails of the corpse, putrefying blood, and voided excrement left open to the air.

Above us in the inky layers of branches the birds began to call, a fast high swell of sound mounting to clash with further waves of chirping in terror and alarm. I saw the kites hovering on outspread wings, wheeling slowly high up in the clouds. I felt rather than saw the electric eyes on watch in the stale thickets of the gardens.

Amm Bashir entered the kitchen with Farag. They carried

the great red chunks, washed and drained of blood, in their arms.

Madame Ulrike was seated at the kitchen door in a cane easy chair with a round cushion on it. She was going to supervise the preparation of supper from the day's catch.

'Amm Bashir,' I said abruptly. 'Where's Rawiya?'

He looked at me with his vague old man's eyes. All the defeat of the world was in those eyes.

'Who is Rawiya, my son? What Rawiya is this?'

Madame Ulrike added quickly 'Which Rawiya, dear? There's no one called Rawiya here. No Rawiya . . .'

Had Rawiya only existed in my imagination?

I know that she was there. What had happened to her?

'Farag! Farag!' I shouted. I was in anguish. 'Tell me! Tell me! Where's Rawiya?'

The boy only looked at me. He did not speak.

That same hunted look I had seen in the eyes of the girl. But his eyes were wet with tears.

Was it she who looked at me from behind the mask?

9

The Indissoluble Music of Salt

How time recedes. It does not exist and never did. Primal innocence: this is the Law.

In a nucleus of being where now there is no trace of what has gone before nor of what will come, I am with her in a café on the Corniche. The pure blue sea with its calm soundless white foam lives on, like youth, unobliterated and inextinguishable. And like youth it is serene, containing not one glimmer of what came after: and there is nothing before.

No 'again' in that sea, nor in she who is with me. Together they are the beginning which does not cease and which is untouched by change. The beginning exists in primacy, without becoming past or present. It is without future.

It is Now. That is all. Without the merest hint of being Now.

A magic wand has wiped the future away – that future which later became past, which later never happened at all.

She was with me. There was peace there, and the shining light of morning.

Her features were not clear. It was as if she were bathed in the silent glow of a radiant cloud.

It was not important – I did not wonder, it did not occur to me to ask – who she was.

I knew her utterly. I was tranquil, content, serene of spirit.

The dream has no time. It is no dream. There is no time.

A sudden breeze blew, refreshing and somewhat chilly, like a challenge.

Then the winter sun ran its fingers through her chestnut-golden hair. One clear beam caught a tendril adrift on the curve of her forehead and made it burst into flame. Her brows were a deep black, her eyes open wide with a hard look in them, a look to shaft my heart and leave it trembling. Eyes brimming with provocative intimations.

'And did I also place eternity within your heart.'

In the wide square outside the main railway station the waiting black carriages have a meaning related to this but incomplete. Processions of arrival and departure, weddings and funerals. The reek of horse stale, standing in yellow puddles beneath the sun.

I heard the hand-press on my way down *shari'* Muharram Bey, the din made by the black iron arm as it rose and fell with a succession of dull thuds. I could see it when I looked through the shop window, past the displays of engineering and law textbooks, volumes on the birth of Islam and the flourishing of the Islamic world, and copies of *Colonialism: the Highest Stage of Capitalism*, translated by Rashid el-Barrawi. When I reached the Café Iskandarani I turned off, without any particular purpose in mind. Perhaps I would go up and call on Hasan Muhammad Hossein; we could go to the cinema perhaps, the Plaza in *shari'* Fuad. I counted the few piastres in my pocket and immediately forgot how many there were.

'Golden eyes at the bus-stop. Tresses swirling with a red-gold fire.

Last night I could not sleep. I was assailed by a tense nervous insomnia filled with reveries and fantasies which made my heart hammer in my chest and my skin slick with sweat. In the nocturnal darkness of the house vague forms filled the air above me and I heard stealthy footsteps and hurried unseen panting breaths. As if I were still that child who saw ghosts as plain as day in the heart of the darkness in

156

all their terrifying manifestations; the long skulls of huge animal heads,
bodies of awesome dimensions but without substance, as if they were
composed of wreathing smoke. Did that child live on imagination
alone? One echoing scream convulses my body which is no longer in
my possession, which can no longer bear the burden of terror. The night
is torn and scattered to the winds, my father and mother come running,
my sisters wake up in alarm. I am still staring, I am aware of that,
eyes fixed willy-nilly and breath snatched away, soaked in a cold sweat
— I know how it pours from me even now. And the spectres are
annihilated as soon as the horror bursts out in that insensate shriek.
Those alien, malformed faces, half-beast, half-demon, still stare at me
from the heart of these nights, their gross bulging eyes unblinking;
featureless faces, expressionless and inhuman but very near — I know
them, these forms, rigid and prodigious enough to stop my very blood
and yet familiar — I have long been intimate with them. The remnants
of that fear endure undecayed, their lees undredged in my soul's core.
Last night my heart was seized more than once by a fearful pounding,
as it used to be in those childhood darknesses with the advent of the
spectres which beset and enclosed me. I deny, I mock, I lie frozen but
the apparitions are the same despots of my spirit as ever they were.
Did I not hear them? Oh, I heard them, more than once I heard
them. There was no doubt in my mind. Stealthy footsteps and panting
breaths and unseen feet thudding. A tumbler fell to roll with a glassy
clatter over the floor but it did not break.'

She told me that the big roomy shelter under the Turkish
building opposite the Cleopatra Café was cold at night. She
said that dear Grandmama had refused to go down there, declar-
ing that the One God had already allotted us our span of years.
In the end they had to collect up the blankets and wrap her
tiny form up in them, and then she bobbed her fluffy white
head and agreed to go down if only so as not to leave them
alone. She also told me that Madame Teresa the Italian lady
and her children, the boy and two girls, had burst into muffled

sobs when they heard the rattle of the anti-aircraft guns, and that when the bombing became intense 'Our Father's' mingled with the Chapter of the Chair from the Quran, prayers in Greek and Italian with cries of 'O Kindly One, O Kindly God Whose Graces are unseen, deliver us from Terror', and that at the end of the raid, heralded by the long joyful wail of the siren, people began to laugh and climb the shelter steps nearly asleep on their feet.

I squeeze my eyes tight shut, I master my breathing, I check the spasms of my blood. I say: It's a breeze blowing in the courtyard, a mouse running perhaps, something like that. But I am not convinced. I am not convinced. Here come the feet again, the panting breaths, the pacing. Nervous insomnia, I tell myself, is an exhausting, insufferable business. And throughout I dream of her. Another waking dream or a dream of sleep? Pleasant in all its bitterness. Why do I deceive my heart? It is she. It is she who awakens my ghosts and my pain. Incessantly and despairingly I dream of her. She is the true despot of my dreams. Of course she knows nothing of all this. Perhaps she is not even aware that I exist at all. And what of that? A classic case of unrequited love: it is known, it is often described, everyone is familiar with it. How cheap it is. Perhaps a multitude of us, a host even, all dream the same dream, and sigh together in the same despair. Lord, what bald, thin stuff this is! How did I ever start it?

At Sidi Gaber, she said, there was a massive rock right out in the sea. They called it 'The Rock of Malta'. They used to have swimming races out to it before returning to the high rugged rocks of the shore. They hunted for crabs, little white ones with transparent legs, by digging out the little crevices deep in the rock where they took refuge. They took thin sticks and poked at the tiny terrified creatures until they were driven scuttling out. The person who collected the most was allowed to be King or Queen of the game and make the others do whatever he or she commanded.

It was Sunday. More exactly it was the second day of the first university term. I did not go to the faculty on the first day. Why was that? What is the importance of that now! The only important thing is that I went into the lecture theatre on the second day of term – and only just in time for the last lecture. I opened the door to find the hall packed with students. It was a lecture on construction engineering and Dr Umar Mamduh was already speaking; he paused as I came in. And then she brought me up short.

I saw her in the first row, in the seat nearest the flight of steps leading up from the centre of the large hall. There was total silence. She was captivating, she bloomed and glowed; her thin dark green sweater was pushed up by her proud bosom, her tumbling hair a red-gold commotion, her face shining through the lecture-theatre air which swirled with near-invisible motes of dust in the afternoon light. She shot a passing glance, no more than natural in the situation, at this new student coming in tardily after the lecture had begun, who was tardy in everything. Alone in the crush of people I climbed the steps and sat down in the topmost row. It had been a meaningless glance, yet I felt my heart plunge and the blood rush to my head. It was then that I had my first taste of the feelings which did not lose their power, not for an instant, through all the endless weeks and months which followed. Her brilliance, her radiance, her glow, the warm effusion of her intrepid vitality! And my darkness, my silence – the fractured entity which was myself, which harboured such unnecessary and incomprehensible agonies, agonies sipped in all their stagnated bitterness.

Really, I say to myself. Shame on you, man! What a way to carry on!

On that same day, that Sunday afternoon, she left the lecture theatre in the ten minutes between the construction lecture and the one on higher mathematics. Heading for the door I drew near her empty seat. I paused by it for a moment. It was hot for October and she had left her jacket on the seat along with a book. In a bold, unconcerned sort of manner I bent to read the title. It was Lamartine, the Selected Poems, *in French.*

It's like a message to me, I thought. Well . . . Fancy that. I was aware of the curious enquiry in the eyes of the surrounding students. I deliberately dawdled on my way out, adopting a kind of despairing droop. Well . . . Good heavens. At no point was I touched by hope, not even for a moment – why? Any kind of hope was rejected forcefully from the beginning. It goes without saying that I dreamed of nothing else but her all day, all week, month, year. Pointless to relate this dream. It is well-known. It has been exhaustively described. Only it had – and still has – a murkiness about it. That and a silence, a silence, a silence. How can this mounting unbroken tumult be a silence whose sting is unabating? How heavily it weighed, the loneliness of this silence. It does so still.

There was a large gecko on the wall, just beneath the ceiling. It was about a foot long, dusty-grey in colour, rock-still, silent and menacing. I could not take my eyes off it. It seemed to be observing me in turn up there. In the morning the Civil Defence Brigade came to the house and distributed gas-masks. I signed a receipt for five. They stank of rubber and the thick perspex over the eyeholes was rather misty. The fat respirator hoses had ringed ribbing. We put them in the loft and forgot about them. After the war we found that the mice had nibbled great pieces out of them and they were encrusted with dry pigeon droppings.

I thought: this is an access of infatuation like all the others – only severer, perhaps, more violent, more terrifying. All those girls! I loved them also in silence. From my lonely cell, I said. As a hermit loves God. It is not a human love, I said, if it can rightly be called love at all, that is. More like a fragment from a pageant of dreams, gorgeous in spite of everything, nightmarish at the same time; a fragment of a lengthy consumptive wasting which finds no flesh to feed on. Bittersweet daydreams, hurts which I almost desire, secret converse I can hardly do without. A flame buried in the soul. A pageant with a will of its own, independent of me, it seems; detached from me. Agonies, ardours, insurrections, always torn and tattered in the end. Coming to mockeries and smiles in the end, ones I imagine to be bitter, from whose tears I know to be bitter.

Why did I not speedily take action? Were we not classmates after all, studying the same subjects in the same faculty? Could we not have simply founded a friendship? Indulged in a bit of blameless sweet-talk, a bit of blameless soul-baring? No. Of course not. What I wanted then – and still want now – was something completely different. Nothing else but that would do. The total granting of the self. The exchanging of that gift where there is neither exchange nor gift, where I becomes You and You, I. I said: How absurd. How puerile. I said; What immolation. What sacrifice . . . I said: The granting of the impossible – an impossible gift. And there was, in fact, another reason. I had actually ventured in my own way already, and already tasted failure. Why do I speak now after all this silence, now that life has ended? Because this has not ended.

On the evening before the Coptic Easter I went to the Globe Theatre at the crossroads of *shari'* Sultan Hossein and *shari'* Safiya Zaghlul. My friend George told me that he would be there at nine. The thick curved glass windows bounding the wide hall were misted with the breath of the crowds of soldiers, officers and other ranks, of every nationality. The smell of beer suffused the deafening bray of the music. The wooden dance floor was crammed with soldiers and their girls, some with dark curls and others blonde, local girls slender or plump and scandalously made-up, clear-skinned ATS girls each one a line of pure poetry flitting through the filthy sweaty alcoholic cacophony, the wild fiesta in the shadow of imminent death in

161

the deserts of Alamein or Tobruk or Bir Hakem. Sylvana's long face, her brown locks fluffed out like the wings of a fan, floated past on the tide. Some of the soldiers were out in the courtyard — I had seen them on my way in — vomiting and pissing shamelessly in the open before making their way back inside, leaning on their comrades or even on their women who had been waiting nearby and shrieking at the sight of men pissing and belching up the contents of thir stomachs. Piercing shrieks they gave — from inebriation and from the giddy surge of sensual release into the parched and hungry reaches of their bodies. I fancied for a minute that I saw, in the cloudiness of some approaching but as yet unrealized future, a look of ultimate and irredeemable despair in the eyes of Sylvana — was it her? I fancied that the waves came crashing in on to the beach at Stanley Bay, that the wind was blowing cold to strike our breasts, that the warm glassbound refuge was lost in a turbid distance. That we were returning from dark high round towers on the rocks of the sea.

And I saw her every day and every day she possessed a vitality more abundant, she was more blooming, more formidable, more beautiful. I entertained myself mightily by observing, surreptitiously and from a distance, the spread of stories, the weaving of rumours, the different flirtations attempted, the various passions kindled, the competitions, alliances and ruptures of which she was the focus and cause. The were only two girls in the class and the other was — of course! — a restrained, reserved, aloof creature who was not beautiful, not even attractive, and did not want to, could not make up for it except by throwing herself into her studies. I observed the looks whose goal and object she was, Norice. Long looks, fleeting looks; sheep-eyed, ardent, smiling looks; contrite, beseeching, challenging ones; grins fixed and forgotten on faces, embarrassed smirks unable to respond; anxious looks, sweet, beguiling, blithe ones, distant ones, ingenuous ones. I observed the faces reddened and beaded with sweat, the faces from which the blood had drained

162

away to leave them white; stormy, lowering, glowering faces, faces masked with indifference. Rivalries followed thick and fast, some covert, some public; insinuations, allegations, veiled backbiting and gibes. From all this I constructed a weird vicarious life, one which I lived in solitude. She fed it all naturally, with a look, a word, a smile, or even by the bold way she walked. With a seemingly involuntary, instinctive guile she fanned this life into a combustion which she fuelled again each time it threatened to wane. I said one time to my friend Hasan Muhammad Hossein, as if I were talking about a girl who meant nothing to me: 'She's dangerous. Sowing love all around her and not reaping a grain of it.' We laughed, and it was almost as if I forgot that I was myself embroiled. But I never forgot, not for a single moment, those long looks she gave me and only me − or so I said to myself. That is true. However much I tried to deny it or interpret it. It is impossible either to deny or to interpret; but it is true.

She told me how they all rallied, boys and girls alike, around the English major who came to the flat belonging to Madame Teresa the Italian lady on the first floor of the house in *shari'* Bubastis. His name was Jimmy. He always took care to bring some highly-valued Nestle's or Cadbury's chocolate from the Naafi, each and every time he came, and he handed it out amongst all the local children.

He was tall and thin in his uniform of navy serge, with a fair moustache and hair which was ever so cropped and trimmed and clipped. He spent the night there; Signor Lafonti, the man of the house, was in a prison camp at Suez. Lafonti used to wear a black Fascist shirt and jodhpurs tight at the calf. He rode an ancient motorcycle which belched out thick smoke and thick roars all down the street. Madame Teresa was plump and slow-moving, and laconic on the few occasions she spoke. As for the two girls and the boy, they had the devil in them and teased all the children in the street.

One night a loud crashing sound was heard in the little

garden directly beneath the verandah. Something must have fallen. What? An unexploded bomb? Impossible; the air-raid siren had not sounded. A gaggle of children, woken by the noise, quickly gathered and in spite of the bellows of the adults rushed out to the little garden in their pyjamas and nightgowns, some slippered and others barefoot. Jumping down from the verandah they found him there on the ground. Stretched out, face tranquil, eyes shut. Major Jimmy's a goner, they said. Dead. They began to scream. No sooner had the grown-ups arrived than they realized that he was simply dead drunk. He had landed on the soft wet ground, bringing a piece of the upstairs balcony with him. 'Madame Teresa!' they called. 'Madame Teresa! Come and help Jimmy! Help us!' They carried him in – he was still unconscious, with a rapturous look on his face – and took him upstairs where they laid him down on Lafonti's bed. He woke up the following morning.

On my first day at the faculty I studied the list, pinned up on the noticeboard, of the students who had been accepted on to the first-year preparatory course. The moment I saw the name 'Ihsan Nasri' I sat up all night writing her what was the first love-letter of my life. It was very polished, very careful of her feelings, and unsigned. I wrote simply that she would know me and that if she read poetry she would know how poets fell in love. I poured my heart out writing of this love of mine which crashed against the boundaries of my heart and gushed over. I sent her the letter. I wrote her name on the envelope, the address of the faculty, the class, everything. I devised long and complicated fantasies about her receiving the letter and seeking out the writer in secret, about the quivering emotions excited in her by the letter – my imagination ran riot. Did her surreptitious glance fall on me? Did she know that I was her unknown admirer? How could all this love emanate from me without meeting any response from her? (This was always one of my favourite fantasies.) Since even if she did not know for certain then she had undoubtedly guessed, guessed with a certainty

164

stronger than any knowledge. Belief in the impossible, then denial of
that belief, time after time without lapsing from the faith. As if apostasy
were part of that faith . . . It was not long before I discovered that
'Ihsan Nasri', though indeed a classmate of ours, was a boy. Eventually
we became firm friends but he never once mentioned the letter. How I
mocked myself, tore myself to pieces. How bitterly I laughed, and
laughed at the bitter laughter. Why didn't I send her another letter,
correctly addressed this time? Why didn't I tell her the whole story?
Undoubtedly we would have laughed together and that would have
cleansed away my agony. I said: No . . . I can only make a single
leap, and then I fall. I said: No . . . even then, she knew. She knew!

It was two in the morning. I was in the flat in *shari'* Ibn Zahar.
The window was tightly closed. I had finished the Luzumiyat
of Abu'l Ala al-Ma'arri and had just gone back to my translation of Shelley's *Skylark* when, at that exact moment, the air-
raid siren went off. The relentless blaring hoots pierced the
nocturnal silence and made my heart pound. Then I heard
the dreadful thump. The walls shook and a flash of white light
filled the inner courtyard of the house, penetrating the bedroom
and the study where my sisters Aida, Hana and Louisa slet
crowded together in the big bed. With the lightning-flash came
the prolonged thunder of collapsing masonry, so near that I
thought for a second that it was our house which had been hit,
but nothing moved. I put on a jacket over my pyjamas and
went out in my slippers. At the top of the street, just at the
end of the side-alley, I saw the house where the man who sold
foul-beans and falafel lived. The front of the house had fallen
away as if it had been sliced off with a giant knife. There was
a heap of mudbrick and other debris in the alley. Each of the
three storeys could plainly be seen in the searchlight beams
raking the pure blue surface of the sky between the clattering
bursts of ack-ack fire, thin and piercing, which exploded to
trail out into green and crimson roses of bursting sparks exactly

165

like fireworks. Beds, cupboards, clothes on pegs along the walls, household clutter. Photographs of the occupants and framed Quran verses, or pictures of St George and of the Virgin in red and blue, still hanging slightly askew on the undamaged inner walls. A small group of men and women stood in nightclothes by the door with their children, the little girls weeping and whimpering, the boys clinging silently to their mothers' skirts, faces white in the night. Suddenly the all-clear sounded, a long happy wail. I went home.

Why do I always curse everyone I love? I curse her all the time. I curse her for the thousands of blissful dreams alive within me still, the fancies wreathed around her, her alone, and for the murderous nightmares which fill my solitude with alarm and pain. I curse her to my own detriment – yet what has she to do with this hysterical tearful laughter? Exactly – I curse her because she is the distant one who knows nothing and is nevertheless not to be blamed because she knows nothing and never will. She will never have so much as an inkling that I went through what amounted to my own Dark Ages in which I created her for myself, in which I plunged through the mire of a forbidden outland. Even now the lady in question knows nothing of this entire story which now appears so trite, so utterly shabby. Yet she herself is unique, exalted, peerless. In Alexandria during the fifties she was a well-known architect, and then I heard no more of her. Of course she never completely disappeared from the sight of that middle-aged man who still loved to envisage upon her face the sediment of many affections. I awoke one day three or four years later and realized all of a sudden that, unknown to myself, my heart had recovered from its passion for her. The paths of the living cross sooner or later; why then did we never meet? Are we dying in life? Lost love, surging to be spilt in vain, unnecessary and meaningless.

A year before this, perhaps two, I had undertaken what was

perhaps one of the rites of the initiation into manhood after the baptism of fire. Into the bottom section of the wooden bookcase which had a glass-fronted upper shelf I disbursed the contents of my adolescence. In the top, behind the panes, I arranged the few books I had: the *Dragon Book of English Verse*, the Torah, the New Testament, the Quran, *The Literature and Religion of the Ancient Egyptians*, *Selected Works of Arabic Poetry*, a *'Selected Just' Arabic Dictionary*, a West English dictionary, a small Belot French-Arabic dictionary which had dried out after a dunking in the Mahmudiya Canal on the occasion of my brief plunge when I failed to step from ferry to shore. Back numbers of *al-Hilal*, *al-Muqtataf*, *Magallati* and *Apollo* magazines which I had bought from the newsagent who spread out his stock on the pavement by the marble wall of the Lebon Company at the end of *shari'* Salah el-Din. I used to run barefoot over the clean warm asphalt of the streets, my sandals under one arm, in pyjamas or tunic, while my mother had her afternoon nap. I had ordered my sisters Aida and Hana to leave the front door open so that I could come back in without knocking. I would return panting, heart beating from the run, the risk, the lucky finds shaking my body, laden with spoils, without my mother knowing that I had gone out at all.

Two wooden boards stuck with mother-of-pearl and sea-shells, big ones and little ones, fetched from the beach the winter before. A white animal skull – a gazelle, or a fox? – with empty clean-smelling sockets, not remotely evil. I had found it on the sandy desert road while working the previous summer with my uncle Nathan. I used to do the wages accounts for the gangs of labourers who were laying the Treaty Desert Road a little way beyond the Rest House. I also registered the sacks of cement and the loads of gravel brought out each day by lorry, writing it all up in duplicate with an indelible pencil. A plaited palm-leaf crucifix taken from the Church of Our Lady in

Muharram Bey one Palm Sunday. An envelope containing strips of gummed paper, a little penknife whose blunted blade had been eaten by rust, an old battered set of shaving tackle, the razor-handle twisted. A half-page 1941 calendar which had been a free gift from *al-Ithnayn wa Kulli Shay' wa'l Dunya* magazine. An advertisement cut carefully out of *al-Balagh* for *The People of the Cave*, which I went and bought from a little bookshop in *shari'* Raghib Pasha for the shocking sum of ten piastres; I kept on at my father until, with a resigned and softhearted smile – a proud one as well – he gave me a big silver coin stamped with seal of Sultan Hossein. A photogravure of Ginger Rogers clipped from *al-Kawakib* magazine, all glossy and blue, her hair metrically shingled, the forerunner of a face which would in coming days become much loved. Two extracts from Baudelaire translated into Arabic which my friend Hani Muhammad Ali had written out in pencil on half a jotter page cut longways. A sheet of blotting paper half-soaked in dry crusted blue ink. A piece of white chalk stolen from school, a broken quill blackened with ink and age, a comb with yellow dusty grains of sand still in its teeth, a nail, a needle, a pencil. An inkstand whose two round hollows contained the traces of red and blue ink, dry now; just the dregs left, coated with a fragile layer of wispy white mould. A piece of cork. A big spiral shell twistily turning which I treasured as well.

Have they all gone, the hoardings of my childhood and early youth?

I had spent an entire year, all except two weeks, as a vegetarian – a rigorous vegetarian, without having studied nutrition or having any real facilities for a change of diet. I simply believed in Abu'l Ala al-Ma'arri, George Bernard Shaw and Gandhi. My father could not accept this stubborn, steadfast, childish deprivation I imposed upon myself. His grief was profound, silent, ultimately destructive. He could not screech one minute and beseech the next the way my mother did, beating her breast in despair and despond as she tempted me with duck she had cooked with couscous: 'the smell will restore you and give you an appetite . . . well at least have a drop of milk at breakfast . . . No? I'll boil you an egg, then – eat, for my sake, my dearest boy, my lamb!'

I held out until just before the celebration of Easter Sunday and the springtime festival of Shamm el-Nessim on the following Monday. The joy in the house was twofold then, but I felt defeated. And my defeat was twofold as well, for I had been vanquished not only by my appetite but also by my love which was still raw and green then. Yet it was mingled with the joy of surrender and the acceptance of the pettiness of reality and its incontrovertible sway.

And at New Year? I must have been in bed, wrapped in blankets and coverlets. I had shut myself in my bedroom in the flat in *shari'* Ibn Zahar. My thick winceyette pyjamas, which I had on underneath the covers, might as well not have been there, so little use were they against the cold. Charcoal was scarce and the kerosene stove hissed away in the room with a bowl of water placed on top to release steam and warmth into the air. The door was left open just a crack against the danger of asphyxiation. Under the covers I was reading *The Intelligent Woman's Guide to Socialism* with as much passion as if it had been a detective story. I could hear the steamers hooting all the way from the Western Harbour to Raghib Pasha, calling and answering each other across the city's nocturnal quiet. Our Greek Orthodox, Italian and Jewish neighbours, plus a few Muslims and Copts, went all together and hurled empty glasses, earthenware pots, cracked china plates and old flowerpots into the road with a joyous smashing. When morning came we would find the wide street carpeted with the shattered fragments of the old year. The Christmas northwesterly had been blowing for the previous three days, since the 23rd of Keyhak; the wind howled and the rain fell in sheets to batter and slap the closed shutters, slackening only to lash the houses anew. Two days before Christmas I had gone down at nightfall to the beach which extended all the way to el-Shatbi and where on my left the waves thundered against the black stones of the sea-wall at Selsela and drews back in a dark blue echoing frothy uproar. The gulls gave broken shrieks as they rose and fell on the wind.

No, I had said. That is enough. This pain cannot go on. Enough.

And I said: This is the beginning of the real comedy, perhaps, or its epilogue; I do not know.

There were three piastres in my pocket and in my soul a bitterness, an anger, a most final resolution.

I said: I must be set free I must smash down the walls the walls of life itself.

Beyond all this lay the perfect void: to my spirit it was perfect repose.

Go then, I said. Off! Away out of the mire of pain and love denied and the compulsion of silence!

How dreadful is this high sea, how strong its siren call. Unmatched sweetness.

Over the wet sands I went, heading for this tomb awash with great gouts of black water. I reached the shoreline, as fixed in aim as if I were in a trance. Only one step more. I said: At that moment I found, amongst the sticky strands of seaweed, a small frightened dragon. I folded it to my bosom and warmed it, I took it back to my room where it grew and grew until its fins were so big they beat against the walls of my house. It sprouted a great many sharp teeth which it embedded in my soul and even now each time one set falls out another grows to replace it. Final time after first time after time. the dragon still appears as the sea floods around me in my turbulent prime teeming with the shades of those beloved in my youth, as living as ever they were, with nothing taken away.

I built the walls in big stone sqaures. They filled up with the choppy waves of the sea. I counted them in my dream – I was fully awake, I was not asleep – and the wall-squares were nine in number. The water gushed in dark volumes over the top of

170

the stones, it brimmed over, the walls could not hold it. Within the nine square walls the new grass had been submerged and the ground stirred up; the tall palms swayed in the teeth of the gale, the furious tempest thrashed and lashed them with a loud voice. In the middle of these squares billowing with brine were sea-creatures, fish-like, humanlike, aquatic; half-woman, half-dragoness. They had a black carapace which seemed as sharp and bristly as coarse sandpaper; it shimmered and then behold, their skins were smooth and golden, their breasts soft but firm and proud. Their heads were curly-haired, raw-boned and rounded; they shimmered and behold, they had silky flowing tresses, wide eyes imbued with womanly tenderness, alluring, calling mournfully as if in an invitation to love, as if they demanded the act of love with no hope of an answer. In this being, this vessel rocking in the water, this ninefold cargo of latent savagery veiled in sweetness and poesy, I run amongst the stone walls flooded with briny swell, I dash desperately down narrow paved corridors where wavelets lap the floor and all the time I hear the hiss of breath from these womanlike sharks these maids of the sea these dragons, genies, sirens, houris whose arms embrace whose sturdy gristlebound flippers strike; these pelican-girls with feathers dripping and waterlogged, these silent, repulsive horrors. And all the time the square walls of stone threaten to collapse under the pressure of the flood I run I want to get out of this wandering maze of criss-crossing corridors where there is no way out save drowning by inches under spouting inrushes of water. I can see no refuge ever I can see no safe dry sunlit place I will never find an escape from this tumultuous interior exterior rumble nor from the tempest reaching the furthest horizon.

When I awoke it was to see the banner headline in *al-Ahram* newspaper. *Fall of the house of Muhammad Ali. Declaration of the Republic: Gamal Abd al-Nasser Deputy Prime Minister and Interior*

171

Minister. He was almost unknown – perhaps also rather hatred at that time, 19 June 1953. We did not know that the day would come when we would sigh for his age and all the glories and trials it brought. The first page of the paper, within a red margin, said that our leader, Chief of Staff Muhammad Neguib, President of the Republic of Egypt, had at one o'clock that morning issued the first Republican resolution, which was to promote General Staff Major Abd el-Hakim Amir the Commander of the Armed Forces to the rank of Major-General. The paper also stated that on that very day there were two flats to rent near the Zoological Gardens, four rooms and six rooms, for eight pounds fifty and ten pounds fifty respectively, telephone no: 97862; and that the price for raw middling American cotton 15/26 ready to be tendered for in England was thirty-two pounds and Egyptian cotton Karnak type 155 was 42 pounds 800 piastres; and a $1\frac{1}{2}$oz. tile of gold in Hong Kong was worth 270.625 dollars, and the value of the Hong Kong dollar was three shillings; and that Dr Isma'il el-Qabbani, the Minister of Education, had accepted from Mr Alfred Bonds of the American Embassy a certificate of honorary citizenship of the state of Arkansas. And that at six o'clock on the evening of the following Monday at the Faculty of Letters in Cairo there would be a discussion of a doctoral thesis presented by Mr Ahmad Muhammad el-Houfi, the subject of which was 'Woman in pre-Islamic Poetry'; and that Neguib el-Rihani's company would perform a play entitled *Son of Whom, May I Ask?*; and that the Metro Cinema here in Alexandria had Robert Taylor and Joan Fontaine in *Ivanhoe* in technicolour.

Cactus thorns filigree wood in intricate smooth and supple lattice; ambiguity incarnate, the lace of her brassière a music pure of symmetry the ripe flesh a hampered outpouring a luscious fruit the body shadowed-illuminated is firm the folds of the cloth floating about it is warm and enmeshing and interlaced the plucking of its fine shivering strings the music of lust no ear can hear.

'What's the matter with you today?' Su'ad el-Samahi asked me. 'You're so quiet!'

'I've got a lot of work,' I replied.

'Poor thing,' she said.

I laughed. In a rather dry, pointed manner I said; 'What do you mean? Incidentally, I don't like pity, not from anyone!'

'Well, that's for the best,' was all she said.

'Nor do I like being buttered up!' I added sharply.

'No, you don't!' she agreed. 'Goodness, you're heated today!' Then I had to make a joke of it. Laughing shamefacedly I put a hand on my forehead and then took my pulse. 'Yes,' I managed at last. 'You're right, madam. I've got a temperature.'

My girl, whom I loved with madness and despair, was silently listening. Then abruptly she spoke. 'You know, you've infected me.'

'Really?' I exclaimed joyfully, and then amended: 'I'm sorry – I'm awfully sorry!'

'What's all this apologizing?' said Su'ad. 'Honestly, go easy, you two!'

She, her, she said plaintively: 'He infected me. I feel cold. And I've got a temperature too.'

'So!' said Su'ad. 'We have a buyers' market here!' She turned to me, laughing. 'The goods are selling, old man! The Lord bring you fortune!'

'Oh, I don't know about that,' I said. I felt embarrassed and frustrated.

As for her, she gave me – as she usually did – an issue of the French magazine *Confidences* which she took regularly. 'All right,' she said. 'Cheer yourself up with a look at some pretty things.'

In the magazine there were pictures of virginal kisses from refined lips, virginal embraces with bodies politely positioned.

Her childlike voice, playful and plaintive, was sweetly musical – how sweet to my ears. My heart beat faster as it usually did.

How dear to me you all are, people of Alexandria.
Between the two shores and the water I adored you utterly.

Your encarmined lips are my lips I stare into your eyes kohled with a deep black and find myself in their depth and the feel of your flowing hair either side of my face the heaviness the volume of your breasts I feel against my chest as your firm plump arms enfold me. I have buried the solid burning column into the warm stuff of tenderness itself which encounters my death and my resurrection together in the profundity of the I is the You I bend all the strength I have to extinguish myself in your body until I and You together finally become that body which is one and indivisible not for one moment not for the blink of an eye can it be sundered I am on the brink of the impossible I will never fall therein belief in the impossible is to deny its existence. It will happen. It has not happened. It is always happening. And it is not ephemeral.

The following day my girl met me by the door of the company building with a morning greeting – '*Bonjour*' – and a look in which I thought I could see a smile. A private message seemed to have passed between us, one in which she seemed to apologise for her silence and to excuse mine as well, mine which had lasted all through the previous day until Su'ad had chivvied us into talking. A look which seemed also to be saying: What to do? When she spoke it was with a hint of tenderness – or so it seemed.

'How are you today?' she said. 'Has your headache gone, from yesterday?'

'Why?' Su'ad asked her slyly. 'Was he ill yesterday?'

'Heavens!' my girl replied, as one conspirator to another. 'Didn't you notice how quiet he was all yesterday? Sulking in a world of his own?'

'And . . . what about it?' I asked.

'Oh, get well. Get well soon,' she said, with a sympathy.

'*Merci*,' I replied. 'Thank you very much' – and was promptly assailed by a bout of mostly nervous coughing.

'Haven't you managed to sell your chill yet?' she asked next.

'No!' I replied meaningfully. 'I can't find anyone to buy it at the moment.'

She laughed. 'Well,' she said deliberately. 'Put it up for auction then!'

'No,' I said. 'I'm selling and that's it. And I've just found a buyer.'

She laughed her quiet, distinctive, musical laugh. However intellectually rigorous I held myself to be, however earnestly earnest, when I heard this music my heart was as unsteady as a child's. I lived on new dreams, fresh ripe dreams now. I hoped for the break of each new day only so that I could see her again. I would rush and hurry through the day all the while dreading its passing, and wait for the coming days with a tremor of alarm, and yet with an unanswerable, irresistible desire. I surrendered to impossibility. I did not accept it. I did not cease in my search for perfection.

Hot blue translucence in the sky's empty heart – it is the heart of the morrow which awaits you. The bread of my coming days is your lips since the black instrument fixes me with its many eyes a small ancient tomb grown about with a trellis of sweet grape-clusters sweet and tart at once and your back recedes in the crowded street and then the world is a sudden void and the tarmac flares into black fire. In the morning happiness lies in the veils of morning mist, my bliss is incalculable and these green waves bubble over into laughter blown by the breath of life with a sunlit heart.

After a short period away I went into the office – and saw her suddenly before me, sitting behind the long curve of the marble-topped desk. She came over to me.

175

'How dare you?' she said. 'You're not upset, are you? *Bonne arrivée* – welcome back . . . Has something happened?'

'No, no, nothing,' I replied. 'A little attack of *weltschmerz*, tht's all.'

'You could have said,' she replied. 'If I'd known I would have come and amused you!'

'No, I don't think so,' I replied, with far too much bitterness. 'But thank you anyway.'

'Never mind.' Her generosity was incomprehensible. 'Insult me all you like, dear boy. You're allowed.'

My heart melted. I wanted to kiss her openly for everyone to see and hang the consequences. I continued to gather gentle words and private looks as if they were pieces of treasure. What wealth. What light. Good tidings sparkling radiant and pure. A sunflower. The beats of my heart, my paces beneath your walls, a cactus in bloom upon your balcony and a smile – a guarded smile – you send to me across the road you dig hollows under my feet you fill the sky in the noonday blue in the glare of the sun where time is lost. The rhythm of the wave again and again opening its arms to fall on to the sand. Returning, returning still, to throw itself upon your breast.

I wandered amongst the old houses around St Joseph's Old People's Home and the Nabawiya Musa School. I suddenly realized that she would disclose her secrets. I could unlock her cipher. The soldiers had pitched their tents in the yard of the Alexandria Secondary School off *shari'* Menaché. They had also set up their guns there.

The demonstrations in Cairo were loud and clamorous. Much later we discovered that they had been planned and plotted and paid-for, and the guns were trained on my heart.

Passion drains away with the sound of the sea through the net of ancient and ornamental lattice shutters. Her small graceful slender-waisted body – the two ends of the fine metal torque around her head could have met and overlapped at her middle – was itself the intricate music, the endless whisper of passions, the drawing back of cloth, the encompassment by the wrung links of a chain. The rain pelts down on the little warm-looking breasts and wooden hands stretch out in agonized entreaty which can never, ever be answered. The fantasies of the music of salt are the single constant, the salt of the shades of both pain and ecstasy is indissoluble. The beats of my heart are a yesterday which has passed away as a painful dream.

Now my dreams hold their breath. Can there be all this joy in the world?

The old echoes are dumb. Utterly dumb.

'The morning of my life is your sleeping face.'

The sun swims through your hair like gold, the boughs of a lilting tree showering dew.

I drink your wine and thirst for ever.

BOSTON PUBLIC LIBRARY

3 9999 03224 707 2

WITHDRAWN

No longer the property of the
Boston Public Library
Sale of this material benefits the Library